THE DUCHESS OF WHISKEY CITY

Book Five
in
The Whiskey City
Series

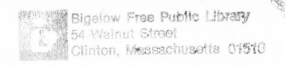
THE DUCHESS
OF
WHISKEY CITY

Book Five
in
The Whiskey City
Series

•

ROBIN GIBSON

AVALON BOOKS
THOMAS BOUREGY AND COMPANY, INC.
401 LAFAYETTE STREET
NEW YORK, NEW YORK 10003

PRINTED IN THE UNITED STATES OF AMERICA
ON ACID-FREE PAPER
BY HADDON CRAFTSMEN, SCRANTON, PENNSYLVANIA

To Will, Odie, Brittany, and Kyle

Chapter One

Two men hunkered themselves down on either side of a narrow trail. Their dirty faces set in grim lines, they trained their rifles down on the ribbon of a trail that cut through the rolling hills.

They had been waiting over two hours and the strain was beginning to take its toll. The tension showed on their faces and in their nervous movements. Finally, the man on the left side of the trail could take the silence no longer. Half-rising from his crouch, he yelled across at his brother. "Hey, Elmo. You still there?"

The sudden sound of the voice startled Elmo, and he jumped, dropping his rifle. "Doggone it, Lester, would you keep still," Elmo hissed, picking up his fallen rifle. "You want to bring every lawman in the country down on us?"

"Oh, yeah, sorry," Lester mumbled, squatting back down. He scrunched up his eyebrows and pursed his lips as he concentrated on staring down the trail. After just a few seconds, he glanced back across the trail. "Say, Elmo," he whispered.

1

"Now, what?" Elmo growled, his patience as thin as the seat of his britches.

"How long we gonna have to wait here? I'm getting downright hungry."

"You're always hungry," Elmo muttered sourly. He sighed and shook his head. He looked to the sky and wondered why he couldn't have been an only child. "The stage'll be by soon. After we do our job, then you can eat all you want."

"I sure wish it would hurry up. I'm getting powerfully hungry. You got anything to eat on you?"

"If you don't shut your yap, I'm gonna come over there and give you a knuckle sandwich to gnaw on," Elmo blustered; for good measure, he picked up a rock and hurled it across the trail. Lester howled and rubbed his ear where the rock hit.

The stage they waited on was still a mile away. The driver, Josh Reynolds, leaned back in his seat, his eyes half closed.

Every once in a while, Josh would open one eye and glance at the boy who was doing the driving. Josh yawned and reflected that it was nice when youngsters rode the stage. First they always wanted to ride up top with Josh, then they wanted to drive. Josh was more than happy to let them. While they drove he could catch a nap.

Josh could tell that this lad knew a thing or two about driving. Not that the job was all that hard; the horses had been down this trail a thousand times and knew the way. Josh took one more peek. Everything was fine.

*   *   *

As the stage rolled innocently into sight, Elmo smiled. This was going to be easy pickings. The driver was asleep and some kid was driving.

Elmo signaled to Lester, then slipped over to his own horse. The plan was for Lester to fire a shot into the air while Elmo rushed the stage. The way Elmo had it figured, the stage would stop and Lester could keep them covered with his rifle while Elmo relieved the passengers of their valuables. Well, it didn't happen quite that way.

Elmo gripped the reins in his teeth, a big pistol in each hand. He stuck his feet straight out, ready to slap the spurs to his horse. As Lester fired his shot, Elmo let out a rebel yell and gave his mount a dose of the spurs. From there everything that could go wrong, did.

Instead of taking off like a shot, Elmo's horse rebelled against the spurs, rearing up and dancing in a circle. Fighting to keep his seat and regain control of the beast, Elmo screamed as he saw that the stage hadn't stopped. Quite the opposite, in fact.

The six horses pulling the stage were spooked by the shot and Elmo's yelling. Throwing their heads in the air, they took off like they'd been struck by lightning.

Elmo finally got his horse pointed in the right direction and pounded down to the trail just in time to see the back end of the stage disappear over the next hill. Choking on the dust and cursing bitterly, Elmo jerked his horse to a stop.

He was still cussing when Lester joined him. Pulling

at the seat of his britches, Lester closed one eye and squinted down the trail. "They didn't stop," he said with mild shock in his voice.

"I can see that!" Elmo snapped, still fuming.

Lester wiped his nose, then spat. He glanced at his brother, then down the trail again. "How come they never stopped? You said they would stop so we could shake the money out of them."

"Shut up, Lester!" Elmo shouted, then threw his hat on the ground. "It weren't my fault. They had some shavetail kid driving. When them hosses spooked, he didn't have enough puddin' in his britches to pull them in."

His long face serious, Lester nodded several times. "Yep, yep. I bet that's right. Say, why you reckon they had a youngster driving the stage?"

"How should I know?" Elmo said with a growl and pounded his fist against the saddle horn. "Pick up my hat," he ordered, shooting a dark scowl down the trail after the stage.

"What are we gonna do now?" Lester asked, dusting off his brother's hat. He spat on the brim, trying to wipe a stain out with his thumb.

"Give me that!" Elmo screamed, jerking the hat from his brother's hand. Fuming, Elmo clapped the hat on his head. "Get your horse. We ain't got time to stand here flapping our gums. John Law is gonna be after us."

As Lester and Elmo rode in flight from the law, Josh Reynolds finally managed to gain control of his horses.

Hauling back on the reins, he shot a hot glance over at young Stevie Hunt. "What in the name of Bessie's bonnet are you trying to do, boy? Kill us all?" he sputtered.

"There was two men! They tried to rob the stage!" Stevie cried excitedly.

Josh snorted and spat over the side of the stage. "My aching backside. You likely seen some poor cowboy out looking for strays."

"No, I didn't. They weren't very good at it, but they sure enough tried to hold us up," Stevie maintained, his lips tight.

Josh laughed and ruffed Stevie's hair. "Tell me, boy. What do you know about robbing stages?" he said kiddingly.

Stevie Hunt placed his knees in the seat and drew himself up as he looked down his nose at Josh. "A lot you know! Me and my sisters robbed a stage one time. We did a better job than those two!"

Josh's head lolled off to the side as he rolled his eyes up at the sky. His laugh was cut off in mid-chortle as a pretty young lady stuck her head out of the stage. Her cheeks were flushed as she smiled up at Josh. "That was a fantastic job, driver," she said, clapping her hands lightly. "You certainly did a wonderful job in thwarting those ruffians!"

"Huh?" Josh grunted, scratching his cheeks vigorously. He stared down at the young lady, a blank look on his face. "Aw . . . well, I reckon that's what the company pays me to do."

"I must applaud your effort. Those men looked like the most unsavory sort," the young lady said brightly.

One thing you had to say for Josh Reynolds, he recovered mighty quick. He wasn't about to let some bottle baby like Stevie Hunt take credit for something good. Josh straightened his collar and beamed down at the young woman. "You got that right, ma'am. Those was some mighty rough characters," he allowed, his chest puffing out a mite. "Now, normally, I woulda stayed and slugged it out with them, but with you along, I figured I best just hightail it. I mean, it wouldn't be right to endanger you. Not with you being a queen and all."

Young Stevie started to protest Josh's boast, but the driver pulled a dollar out of his vest pocket and held it back to the youngster. "Keep quiet kid," Josh said out of the corner of his mouth. As Stevie greedily took the money, Josh shoved him away, then whipped off his hat. "Yes, ma'am, I reckon it's a real honor to save the life of a queen."

The young lady's cheeks glowed bright pink as she saluted Josh. "You're most gallant, sir, but I'm not a queen. Just the daughter of the czar."

"Makes no difference to me, Miss Catrinia. In my book, you're a queen, all the way," Josh declared, grinning so hard he almost swallowed his tobacco.

While Josh choked and clawed at his throat, Bertha Briscoe heaved herself out of the stage. She jerked her dress down and looked up at the driver's seat for her stepson. "Stevie, are you all right?"

Stevie scrambled across the top of the stage, grinning down at her. "I'm fine," he assured her, his grimy fingers hugging the dollar.

Satisfied that Stevie was fine, Bertha turned her attention to the driver. "Hey, logjam, you gonna sit there all day sucking in flies, or are you gonna move this crate?"

His face pale and contorted, Josh nodded weakly. "Yeah, if you folks wanna settle back into your seats, I'll check the horses, then we'll be moving."

Josh gave Catrinia one last smile, then jumped down from his seat. He hiked his britches up, then strutted up to the head of the team. He smiled at the lead horse, the grin stretching plumb across his face. Imagine that—he, Josh Reynolds, had just saved the life of a princess or whatever the devil Miss Catrinia was.

Josh licked his lips. It just dawned on him that saving the life of a princess was surely worth one fat reward. Already Josh had forgotten the fact that Catrinia hadn't been in much danger and that he had been asleep when it happened. In Josh's mind, he'd just saved the princess from unspeakable dangers.

Thinking about it, Josh's smile deepened to the point that it hurt his cheeks. Part of it was the reward, but part of it was the princess herself. Catrinia Romanov was not only a lovely young woman, she had also shown herself to be kind and considerate—not at all like the crabby, snooty picture Josh had always seen when he thought of royalty.

Happy as a hog in mud, Josh finished checking the horses, then started to crawl up in his seat. He was just about to swing into his seat when something slugged him hard in the wind. He toppled over backward, hitting the hard ground flat on his back. He never heard the echo of the shot rolling through the hills. Or the ones that followed.

Chapter Two

A body can just take so much, and let me tell you, I was just about at the end of my rope. Fact is, I was just about ready to bust loose and mash somebody's head.

Now, my two chief tormentors were Iris Stevens and some danged big Russian. That Russian, his name was Arkady Rostov and he had himself some fancy-pants title. Chief of the Royal Palace Guards or some such nonsense. Now, I had another name for him. 'Course, it wasn't nearly so highfalutin. Although it sure enough had the word *royal* in it.

You see, we had the daughter of a czar coming to Whiskey City. The old gal had herself a fancy moniker too. Grand Duchess Catrinia Romanov. I could just picture what a Grand Duchess would look like, gray-haired, wrinkled up and sour as spoilt cider.

I wasn't in any hurry to see her. Not so with the rest of the town, they couldn't wait. Rostov and Iris—shoot, practically the whole blamed town—thought we needed to gussy the place up for her. Since I was sheriff, I got nominated to do the work.

Now me, I had no earthly idea what the devil a czar was and cared even less. I figured if this old gal was too good to see Whiskey City the way it was, she best stay where she came from.

'Course, my opinion was on the dry side of the creek. The rest of the town was tickled pink that she was coming. Today, they were all in a tizzy. You see, the old hide was coming in on the stage this very day. The town had all sorts of big doings planned. Why, they had enough food fixed to feed half the West. Too bad things didn't go to plan. I was sure looking forward to wrapping my choppers around some of that food.

The first clue we had that things had gone wrong was when the stage team came trotting into town without the coach or any of the people. Now, I reckon them fool horses had pulled that stage into Whiskey City so many times that they didn't need a driver. I mean, they went to the Burdett's stable, happy as larks. They sauntered up to the stable like they expected to be fed.

I never got to see any of this. I was down at the other end of town, slappin' paint on a hitching rail, with Iris watching my every move. When Burdett spied them horses, he let out a beller that sounded like a bear with a sore behind.

When I heard that yelp, I liked to have jumped outta my skin. I whirled around and somehow managed to splatter paint across Iris's face. That old bat snatched in a hard breath and her eyes shot lightning bolts my way. I swear, her face turned redder than the paint, and I knew I was about to get my tail twisted.

The only thing that saved me was that Burdett was still screaming to high heaven. "Teddy, get down here. Something bad's happened to the stage!" the burly blacksmith yelled.

Right then and there, I knew that whatever problem the stage had, I'd sooner deal with *it* than with old Iris. Fact is, I'd rather rassle a catamount in an outhouse than take on that old woman.

Well, what I did was slap that paintbrush in her hand, mumble an apology, and take off at a high gallop. Now, the way Burdett was yelling, I s'pect they could hear him way down in Texas. I know Arkady Rostov heard from inside the hotel. That big Russian busted outta the hotel like a boulder going over a cliff.

I had a good head start on Rostov, and still, he like to beat me down to the stable. When we skidded to a stop in front of Burdett, I was huffin' and puffin' like a leaky steam engine and Rostov hadn't even mussed a hair.

Rostov placed his hands on his hips. "The stage," he said thickly, his eyes boring into the smith, "what happened to the stage? The Grand Duchess was on that stage!"

Burdett frowned up at the Russian, then spat on the ground. "Shoot, I know that," Burdett said, growling sourly. "Why do you think I was calling for Teddy?"

By then, I'd sucked up enough wind that I could at least talk. "What did happen to the stage?" I managed to ask between gasps.

Dead serious, Burdett ran a finger along his jaw and

shrugged. "Don't rightly know," he admitted, then waved a hand at the team. "But them cayuses lumbered in without the wagon. I don't reckon that's a good thing."

"A very astute observation, especially for one with your limited mental capacity," Arkady Rostov rumbled as I took a gander at the horses.

Now, I ain't rightly sure what Rostov said, but I reckon the gist of it was that Burdett was a dunce. The same thing musta dawned on Burdett, 'cause his mouth fell open and his wad of tobacco rolled out onto the ground.

"Why you big . . . you can't talk to me thataway," Burdett sputtered, then whirled to me. "Teddy, did you hear what he said?"

"I'm busy," I growled, stooping down to peer at the broken and splintered drawbar, which hung loosely from the harness. As I studied the thing, I saw something that gave me the jeebers.

While I gaped at that drawbar, Burdett stooped down and picked up his wad, dusting it off as he inched backward. He pointed a gnarled finger at Rostov. "You're lucky my elbow is all stove up, or I'd make you eat them words," the smith mumbled.

Looking impassively down at Burdett, Arkady Rostov pulled at his beard, then grunted something in Russian. He turned to me and folded his arms across his broad chest. "There has been trouble with the stage?" he demanded as a crowd of folks gathered around.

"I'd say so," I replied, holding up the bullet I'd just dug out of the shattered drawbar. "That didn't come out of a slingshot," I added, passing the slug to the Russian.

Rostov turned that slug in his hands, then passed it back. He whirled to Burdett. "Saddle my horse," he said to the smith, then stabbed a finger at Joe Havens, who'd come from the saloon to see what all the ruckus was about. "You, go to my room and bring me my rifle," Rostov barked, then spun back to me. "If you can show me the route the stage took, I'll be on my way."

I stood up slowly, closing my knife and sliding it back into my pocket. I stared at the big Russian, and believe me, I never cared for the way he was throwing his weight around. "Ain't no sense in going off half-cocked. I'll mosey out and see what the problem is," I informed him.

Now, that big Russian swallowed that bit of news like it was a raw egg. "Catrinia is my responsibility. I will do this," he allowed, then glared at Joe, who hadn't even turned a hair, much less galloped off to fetch the rifle. "I told you to retrieve my weapon from the hotel," Rostov said, his tone icy as a polar bear's whiskers.

It didn't bother Joe any. He sneered and thumbed his nose at that Russian. "I never took you to raise. You want your shootin' iron, you can just hustle over there and fetch it your ownself."

For a second, I thought Rostov was gonna pop at the seams. He was durn near snortin' fire as he pulled himself up to his full height. Sputtering in Russian, he cocked back a fist the size of a weaning hog.

Most days, I woulda enjoyed a scrap, but today I already had a full kettle of fish, and I sure didn't need more trouble. I stepped between them, shoving Rostov back a step, and believe me, that chore took a little elbow grease. "No need to start a row," I said, trying to make it sound firm. "Rostov, you want to come with me to check out the stage, that's fine. You go fetch your rifle and I'll give Burdett a hand with the horses."

Rostov didn't like it, not one bit, but when I pointed out that we were burning daylight, he went off without a scrap. Breathing a sigh, I trotted into the stable. I swear, keeping the lid on a place like Whiskey City was like herding hogs, a body best keep on his toes at all times.

I didn't really want that sour Russian along, but I had a sneaky suspicion that gent was rougher than an outhouse corncob. If we ran into trouble, he might come in handy.

By the time me and Burdett got the saddles snapped on the horses, the big Russian was back and rarin' to go. Without a word, he swung onto his horse and rode out of the stable.

Burdett spat and kicked dirt at the heels of Rostov's horse. "I swear, that hombre is 'bout as friendly as a wolf with a bad molar."

In all his born days, I don't reckon Burdett ever said anything that was closer to the truth. I just didn't know that before everything was all said and done, I'd be glad that Rostov had such a nasty disposition.

My mood was sour as spoilt grapes by the time I caught up with Rostov. I can tell you, I surely wasn't looking forward to spending a day with a surly cuss like him.

Together, we backtracked the stage team in total silence. A couple of times, I tried to strike up a conversation, but all Rostov did was grunt back at me, so I gave it up.

The trail was easy to follow and after a couple of hours we came on the coach. The stage lay beside the road, tipped over on its top. Sprawled beside the coach was the stretched-out body of a man. Even from a distance, I could tell the body was that of Josh Reynolds. I recognized that red checkered shirt Josh favored.

Reacting as one, me and Rostov slapped the spurs to our mounts. We barely made two jumps before the bullets started hailing down around us.

When Catrinia Romanov woke she couldn't remember what had happened to her. Slowly the memory of the shots and the stage wreck flooded back into her mind. Still, she couldn't figure out where she was. All she knew was that her head was pounding. Very quickly, she discovered her hands were tied.

Fear shooting through her, Catrinia looked quickly around. A fire burned a few feet away. A coffeepot and skillet sat on the fire, but as far as Catrinia could tell, no one was tending them.

As much confused as scared, she tried to sit up, calling

out into the gathering darkness. "Hello, is anybody there?"

"Lady, if you know what's good for you, you'll sit still and keep your mouth shut," a cold, almost jeering voice said.

Her heart feeling as cold as that voice, Catrinia twisted her head around to look at the owner of the voice. He was a tall, rangy man, who moved with slow, fluid grace as he crossed to the other side of the fire.

"Who are you? What are you going to do to me?" Catrinia asked, holding her breath as she shrank away from him.

The man stooped down, stirring whatever he was cooking in the skillet. As he looked up, he smiled tauntingly across the fire at her. "My name is Ferrell Cauruthers."

"What are you planning to do with me?" Catrinia asked, a catch in her throat.

Cauruthers rubbed the three-day growth on his hollow cheeks and looked frankly at Catrinia. Finally, he shrugged and poured himself a cup of coffee. "To tell the truth, I don't rightly know," he replied, his eyes staring into his cup. "I was just told to nab you and bring you here," he explained. He took a sip of coffee, then glanced across the fire. When he spoke his voice was harsh. "We'll be here a couple of days. As long as you don't give me any trouble, you might just live to tell about this. You cross me or try to get away, and you'll regret it dearly."

Chapter Three

Lester slurped from his canteen, looking back over his shoulder. "You think we lost them?" he asked.

"How in the blazes am I supposed to know?" Elmo sputtered, ripping the canteen from Lester's mouth, nearly taking a couple of teeth along for the ride. Elmo dribbled water down his chin and the front of his shirt as he sucked noisily on the mouth of the canteen. After he drank his fill, Elmo tossed the canteen carelessly in Lester's direction and wiped his mouth on the back of his hand. "We sure enough made our trail mighty dim, but now ain't the time to get soft."

"What do you mean?" Lester asked sourly as he rubbed the side of his face where the canteen thumped him.

"That Sheriff Cooper. Now, he's a right hard man. I calculate he'll be looking for us. We best do something awful slick to throw him off our trail."

Lester bit off a piece of jerky. He chewed loudly and nodded his head several times. "Yep, I reckon you're right as rain. Whatcha got in mind?"

Elmo smiled and slapped his brother across the back. "The way I see it, that sheriff is gonna expect us to scat up in the hills and hide out," Elmo said, a slow grin breaking across his long, horse face. "Now, I reckon that sheriff will chase up there after us."

Lester didn't share his brother's glee. A frown on his face, he wrinkled up his nose and stared longingly up at the mountains. "That's likely. We best scram 'fore he ketches us."

Elmo laughed and shook his head. "No, no. That's the last thing we want to do."

"Huh?" Lester whined. "You got the fever or something? You ain't makin' sense," he said blankly.

" 'Course I'm making sense," Elmo replied smugly. "Sheriff Teddy will expect us to head for the hills, but we'll circle around and head the other way."

"That'll take us right into Whiskey City," Lester worried. His face stone serious, he grabbed his brother's arm. "Elmo, they don't like us there."

"Who gives a hoot about that? We ain't fixin' to move there and join the church." Elmo licked his lips and rubbed his hands together. "That sheriff is gonna be chasing us all over the mountains and that fat bank is gonna be just setting there. We could take the place and get away scot-free."

Lester was a long ways from being convinced. "What about that old gal, Iris? She done said she'd shoot us on sight the next time she saw us. Elmo, that old bag is meaner than a hat full of rattlers!"

Elmo snorted and waved a careless hand in his brother's direction. "Don't worry, no one will even know we're about. We'll slip in at night and rob the bank and slip out. They won't be able to get a posse up until the sheriff gets back, and by that time we'll be long gone."

Now, I don't know if you ever jumped headfirst off a horse that's going flat out, but take it from me, it ain't a pleasant experience. I hit facefirst and skidded a good ten yards.

Somehow, in all of that, I managed to haul out my shooter and get it guided in the direction of the stage. I pointed that hogleg at the stage, but I didn't shoot. Instead, I hollered across at them. "Hold your fire! This is Sheriff Theodore Cooper of Whiskey City."

As my words died away the shooting came to a ragged halt. "Teddy? Is that you?" a vaguely familiar feminine voice called out cautiously.

Maybe that voice sounded a little familiar, but I wasn't near ready to rush out and give her a bear hug. At that moment I was hunkered down behind a big rock, and considering the way the lead had been flying, I was right comfortable. "Yeah, it's me, Teddy. Who are you?" I called out.

"It's me, Bertha Briscoe. Preacher Tom's wife."

Like I didn't have enough troubles! I collapsed down to the ground and let out a heartfelt groan. Bertha Briscoe! Great spotted ghost! To tell the truth, I'd rather it woulda been a nest of killers and cutthroats. "You got them kids with you?'' I asked, already dreading the answer.

My answer came in the form of little Jenny Hunt running around the corner of the stage, her pigtails flapping. ''Uncle Teddy!'' she cried, skipping over to me. I'd just started to climb to my feet, when she bowled into me, throwing her arms around my neck and knocking me back on my saddle shiner. ''I missed you!'' she cried, then went and planted a slobbery kiss on my cheek.

''Yeah,'' I said, shying away as I rubbed the slop off my face. To tell the truth, I'd just as soon wrap my arms around a polecat as some kid. Especially a squirmy, gabby one like Jenny. What was worse, I knew she wouldn't be alone. She had an older brother and sister, and they were like rain and mud. Where you found one, you found the other. I swear, just being around them made me nervous as a man with dynamite under his bed.

As the others came from behind the stage, Rostov climbed slowly to his feet. He saw that Bertha and little Stevie Hunt still had their rifles, and he jabbed his own rifle at them.

Now, I'll admit that just for a second, I was tempted to let that big Russian blast them. Especially when Joan Hunt waved and grinned at me. Joanie was just becoming a young woman, and believe me, that girl had notions. I felt the temptation and fought it off. ''It's okay. They're on our side,'' I said, setting little Jenny on her feet and getting to my own.

His bull head jutting forward, Rostov glared at the

passengers. "What has happened here? Where is Duchess Catrinia?"

It was Bertha Briscoe who answered. "They took the princess," she said, leaning her rifle against the stage.

"Who took her?" I asked, taking my hat off as I bent over the prone Josh Reynolds. The stage driver had been shot low down on the left side of his chest.

"I don't know who they was," Bertha answered, pushing a sweaty lock of hair out of her face. "They hit us twice."

"Twice?" I echoed, relieved to see Josh was still alive and that his wounds had been tended and bandaged.

Bertha shrugged. "The first time, Josh must have been ready for them. We took out like a shot and outran them."

"I was driving at the time," little Stevie Hunt claimed, holding his rifle proudly.

Bertha frowned at Stevie, irked that he interrupted her, I guess. "While we was waiting for the horses to catch their breath, they attacked us again. Before we even knew what was happening, they shot poor Josh."

Bertha paused, pointing to a man back down the trail a few feet. "That nice Russian gentleman shot out of the stage like he had a spring in his drawers. He put up a fine scrap, but they gunned him down, and then the horses spooked. We got this far before the stage tipped over."

I don't reckon Rostov was listening anymore. He walked stiffly back down the trail to where the fallen man lay. "Nikolai!" he exclaimed softly. He bent down beside the man, examining him gently.

Arkady Rostov looked up, cold fury and sorrow fighting for control of his face. "This man is dead!"

Bertha nodded grimly. "Yeah, I did all I could for him, but there wasn't much chance." Then Bertha surprised me. I always figured her to be a mighty coarse woman, but she was being tender as she touched Rostov's shoulder lightly. "I never knew your friend long, but he seemed like a mighty fine man. He died brave and true."

Her tenderness ran off Rostov like rainwater off a tin roof. He stood up, his slablike face bleak as an alkali flat. "Where are the other men who guarded the princess?"

Bertha shrugged. "Weren't no other men with her. Just that Nikolai feller."

For a second, pure shock flooded across Rostov's face, then he abruptly turned and stalked stiff-backed to his horse. "Hey, wait a minute," I called after him. "Where are you going?"

One foot in the stirrup, he turned to look back at me, his eyes bright and hard. "I am going after the duchess."

"Josh is still alive," I protested. "I'm going to need your help and your horse to get him and the rest of these folks into town."

Rostov shrugged, an almost elegant gesture for a man of his bulk. "They are peasants and unimportant. My duty is to Miss Catrinia."

"No," I said flatly. "You're gonna help me and these folks whether you like it or not."

Rostov dropped his foot out of the stirrup. He placed both feet squarely underneath him as he faced me. "These people are of no concern. Czaritsa Catrinia's safety is the only important thing now."

"I don't see it that way," I said firmly. I met his gaze, hoping if I gave him a minute, the big Russian would come around, but he wasn't about to budge. He didn't, so I got jaw-to-jaw with him. "Like I said, I don't see it thataway, and since I'm the law in these parts, what I say goes."

Rostov placed both hands on his rifle, holding it across his chest like he was of a mind to use the thing. "I do not believe you can stop me," he threatened. Believe me, even though he didn't raise his voice it was an honest-to-goodness threat.

I almost smiled. He just thought I couldn't. Now, maybe Mr. Arkady Rostov was a rough man where he came from, but out here, he best learn to point that rifle 'fore he started running his jaw.

My hand swooped for my pistol, snapping the weapon up and gouging him in the gizzard with the barrel. I have to say, I snatched that hogleg mighty quick. Rostov never even had a chance to blink. If I expected Rostov to fall to his knees blubbering, I was in for a rude shock. The big Russian just stared at me. "You won't shoot," he said calmly.

Well, he was right about that. To tell the truth, I didn't

have the foggiest notion what to do next. I didn't want to drill the Russian, but I couldn't let him leave. I needed the big Russian, and I especially needed his horse.

Out of the corner of my eye, I could see Bertha shooing the kids back behind the stage. Right then I decided to change my tactics. If you're trapping and you ain't catching anything, you change the bait.

"Look, if those men meant to harm your duchess, they've already done it. Ain't a thing we can do about it now. Besides, it's gonna be dark in less than an hour. No chance of doing much to catch them until morning. You help me get these people into town, and come morning, I'll help you fetch the old gal home."

For a long minute, Rostov's expression didn't change and he didn't move, then suddenly, he set down his rifle and crossed to the stage. "We can use this to carry my fallen comrade and the wounded man?" he asked.

I nodded; that's what I'd had in mind. Both me and Rostov are big men, and we had little trouble flipping that coach on its wheels. One thing you gotta say for Rostov, when he made up his mind to do something, he wasn't bashful about putting a little sweat into the job. He rigged a makeshift hitch and hooked our two horses up to the stage, and Bertha and the kids helped me ease Josh into the stage.

We put the dead Russian in with him; then, with the rest of us walking, we set out for town. Rostov led the horses, and I carried young Jenny Hunt. We didn't make good time. Everybody was tired and two horses were a bit light to pull the stage, so we took it slow.

It was way past dark when we made it to town. The minute we crossed into town, Bertha took charge. She shooed them kids off in the direction of the hotel, then put me and Rostov to the job of packing Josh to the hotel.

Now, after we got Josh bedded down and Bertha tending him, I figured to catch some sleep and go after the princess first thing in the morning, but Rostov would hear nothing of that.

He insisted that we snag a couple of fresh horses and scoot out to where the holdup took place. He figured we could get on the trail at first light thataway. I reckon he was right, but I was bushed. I coulda used some sleep, but it wasn't to be. My tail dragging lower than a bottom plow, I gave up and followed the big Russian out of town.

From the top of a hill just outside of town, Elmo and Lester watched. They saw the stage come in and then watched as Rostov and Teddy rode away.

Lester scratched his head and stared blankly at his brother. "How come the stage is just now getting into town?"

For an answer, Elmo swore and slammed his hat down on the ground. "We shoulda chased after the stage," he complained bitterly.

Lester's scratching became more vigorous as he tried to follow Elmo's line of thinking. "Well, I guess they went slow enough that we sure coulda caught them, all right," he said slowly. "But you always said we had to take them by surprise to rob a stage."

" 'Course you got to take them by surprise!" Elmo snapped. "That driver carries a scattergun. You don't sneak up on them and the undertaker will be a month digging the buckshot outta you."

"Sure, sure," Lester agreed, his head bobbing up and down. "But if we couldn't take them by surprise, why would we want to catch them?"

Elmo swore again and kicked his hat. "Lester, I swear, sometimes you're denser than an adobe brick. Didn't you see the way the top of the stage was all busted up and they was a couple of horses shy?" he asked, and Lester bobbed his head attentively. "The way I figure it, that goofy driver went and wrecked the stage."

All of a sudden, Lester's face lit up like a birthday cake, and he jumped up and down, shaking his finger. "You know, if we woulda follered them, we coulda took their money while they were getting their senses back after the wreck!"

Elmo groaned and rolled his eyes up at the star-filled sky. "That's what I've been trying to tell you. Now, would you shut up so I can think?"

With that Elmo begin to pace, with Lester dogging his every step. Elmo tugged at his ear and stared up into the sky as he paced. All of a sudden he stopped, snapped his fingers, and pointed at Lester. "I've got it!" he exclaimed.

"Got what?" Lester said, grunting.

"A plan," Elmo said, waving frantically for his brother to come closer. Elmo looked both ways into the darkness, then leaned into Lester and whispered. "We just saw the sheriff leave town, so all we gotta do is wait till the rest of the folks go to sleep. Then we slip down, jimmy the back door of the bank, and take the money."

"I dunno," Lester mumbled. "It's been my experience that them banks keep their money in one of them safes. How we gonna get the money out?"

Elmo shook his head sadly. He made a *tsking* sound and patted his brother on the back. "It's so simple. We just shoot the lock off."

"Oh, yeah," Lester replied, a smile growing on his face. "Well, I reckon all we gotta do now is wait for them folks to go to bed," he decided, and began to gather some sticks.

"What the blazes are you doing?" Elmo demanded, hand on hips.

Lester dropped his sticks, looking guiltily at his brother. "I was gonna build a fire and make some coffee while we wait."

About half of the scream poured past Elmo's lips before he could get them clamped shut. He started to whip off his hat and whack Lester with it, then realized he wasn't wearing his hat. Grinding his teeth, he settled for kicking dirt. "Are you crazy? You want to bring the whole town up here?"

"Well, I'm hungry," Lester complained. "I could use a cup of coffee too."

"You're always hungry," Elmo accused. "Just sit quiet. After we hit this bank, you'll have enough money to buy yourself an eating house and eat all you want."

"Really?" Lester asked, smacking his lips. "Could I get a cook to make me an apple pie every day?"

"If that's what you want."

"Boy, yeah!" Lester replied. As they waited and the lights slowly went out in Whiskey City, Elmo had to endure listening to all the refinements Lester was going to put in his eatin' house. By the time Whiskey City lay in total darkness, he was sick of it.

Elmo waited a few minutes after the last light went out, then climbed to his feet. "Lester, let's go," he said with a growl.

"Huh?" Lester grunted, coming slowly out of his daydreams. "Where we going?"

"To rob the bank, you fool!"

"Oh, yeah, right," Lester recalled. "I'm still hungry, though," he commented as they tightened their cinches and prepared to move out.

Elmo sighed and looked up at the sky, wondering what he had ever done to deserve being saddled with an affliction like Lester.

It was deathly still as they rode into Whiskey City. The stillness gave Elmo the creeps. It seemed like the whole world was just holding its breath.

Looking all around, they circled around, coming up to the bank from the rear. They stopped in the alley behind the bank and Elmo sat on his horse, rubbing his hands together. "Oh, boy, we're gonna be rich," he squealed.

They left their horses ground-hitched and slowly sidled up to the bank. Elmo tried the back door; as expected, it was locked.

"What are we gonna do about that?" Lester asked, then hauled out his pistol and held it up. "I could shoot the lock off," he suggested eagerly.

Elmo cocked his head off to the side and rubbed his chin. "No, we'll just break it down," he decided. "That'll be quieter. Stash that hogleg and break down the door."

"Gotcha," Lester replied, slapping the pistol back down in the holster. He backed off a good twenty paces, then licked a finger. He held the finger up, testing the wind.

"Would you hurry up?" Elmo whispered urgently.

"Yes, sir," Lester said. He squinted one-eyed at the door, then slid a couple of paces to the left. He scraped his feet into the dirt, then rocked back and forth several times. Finally, with a little yell, he charged. His legs pumping like a butter churn, he barreled full blast into the door.

That door didn't even have the decency to groan a mite. It held its ground and Lester bounced off like a moth hitting an oak tree. Howling in pain, Lester careened backward, landing on the seat of his britches. He flopped around on the ground, cussing and holding his injured shoulder.

Horrified, Elmo mostly managed to bite off the scream that welled up in his throat. Waving his arms frantically, he rushed over to his brother's side. Dropping to his knees beside his fallen brother, Elmo clamped a rough hand over Lester's mouth. "Would you quit your yowling! You want to bring the whole blamed town down around our ears?" Elmo demanded, far more concerned with the noise than the fact that his brother might be hurt.

"But my arm hurts something awful," Lester whined.

"If you wake up this town, you're gonna be hurting from head to toe," Elmo threatened. "That old bat with the buffalo gun hears you and you'll wish you were never born. You wanna see her again?"

"Iris?" Lester whispered the name with reverence, then shook his head emphatically. "I don't ever want to see that old hag again!"

"Then pipe down and keep your yap closed."

Big tears welled up in the corners of his eyes, but Lester clamped his mouth shut and clutched his wounded shoulder quietly. A deathly silence slowly crept over the town. In the silence, the distinctive sound of a gun being eared back to full cock rang out clearly. Both Elmo and Lester heard it and froze in their tracks.

Chapter Four

Without a word, Lester and Elmo threw their hands into the air. They cocked their heads forward, trying to see through the gloom of the alley. No matter how hard they tried, they couldn't see into the shadows where the man with the gun stood. "I hope it isn't that old battle-ax with the buffalo gun," Lester worried, fidgeting from side to side.

"Shut up," Elmo hissed out of the corner of his mouth. He smiled sheepishly and took a step forward. "Listen, we wasn't doing no harm. We was just looking for a nice quiet place to bed down," he said, spreading his hands innocently in front of him.

"Looked like you was trying to break into the bank."

"Crimany, it's just a young 'un!" Lester exclaimed as young Stevie Hunt stepped out of the shadows.

"Not only that, it's the brat who was driving the stage," Elmo sputtered, then gaped as little Jenny stepped up beside her brother. "Oh, no, there's two of them."

31

"She's my little sister," Stevie declared, still pointing the pistol at the pair.

"You're a little young to be packing a shootin' iron," Lester said, scratching his head. "Where'd you get that thing?"

"It belongs to Mr. Reynolds the stage driver. I'm holding it for him until he gets to feeling better," Stevie replied, running his finger along the barrel. "You guys want me to show you how to get into the bank?"

His face bland, Elmo shook his head. "You got it all wrong, sonny. We weren't trying to bust into the bank. We was looking for a place to bed down for the night."

Little Jenny Hunt put her tiny fist on her hips and stared sternly at the pair. "Well, why didn't you just go to the hotel?"

"Hotel rooms cost money. We don't have any," Elmo replied smoothly.

"Wouldn't it be nicer in the stable where there's some straw to sleep on?" Stevie asked.

Holding a finger in the air, Lester turned to face his brother. "You know, Elmo, maybe we could stay in the hotel. It sure would be nicer than sleeping out here on the hard ground."

Elmo swore and shook his head. "Lester, you dang fool! We ain't here to bed down. We're here to rob the bank!"

"Oh, yeah," Lester said, a note of wonderment in his voice that wilted under his brother's severe frown. "Sorry, I forgot," he mumbled.

Stevie laughed. "I told you so," he said. A smirk riding on his face, the youngster leaned against the building. "I can show you how to get in," he offered.

Elmo hooked his thumbs in his suspenders, puffing out his chest as he pulled himself up to his full height. "We don't need any help, thank you very much." Elmo sniffed and snapped his suspenders a couple of times. "I'll have you know, me and Lester is professionals. We pulled some mighty big jobs in our time."

"Me and my sisters pulled some jobs ourselves," Stevie told him.

"Yeah, sure," Elmo snorted. "Now be good little kids and stand back so we can work," he said, shooing them back. Stabbing a finger at his brother, Elmo jerked his head in the direction of the door. "Lester, break it open."

"That door is pretty thick. It looks new too. I bet it'll be tough to knock down. I can show you an easier way," Stevie offered.

"You should listen to him," Jenny said, pointing a scolding finger at Elmo. "Stevie's real smart."

Elmo swore softly and rolled his eyes. "We're pretty smart ourselves. Now shut up," he sputtered, then stabbed a finger at the door. "Break it down."

His face sour, Lester took a long step back and rubbed his shoulder. "Maybe we ought to listen to him. My shoulder still aches something fierce from the last time."

"Why, you little Milly," Elmo muttered. "I'll just have to do it myself," he said and backed off a step or two. He charged that door like a runaway buckboard, but his results were remarkably similar to Lester's. Sitting on his keister and holding his throbbing shoulder, Elmo looked up at Stevie. "Show us what you had in mind," he said in a small voice.

Stevie smiled and flipped the gun down in the holster, which hung down to his knee. He walked over to the tiny window in the rear of the bank. He smirked back at Elmo, then slid the window open. "There you go."

Elmo climbed triumphantly to his feet. He smiled and patted Stevie on top of the head. "Well, sonny, I reckon you did your best, but I'm sorry to say there ain't no way we're gonna fit through that window," he said, but he didn't sound at all sorry. Not judging by the grin plastered clear across his face.

"No, I don't reckon you can fit, but she can," Stevie replied, pointing to Jenny. "She can crawl through the window, come around, unlock the door, and let us in," he added, making a big show of explaining it.

Growling to himself, Elmo kicked dirt. Dad-gummed, snot-nosed, little pony rat! Elmo had a notion to wring his scrawny little neck. The thing was, he also wanted in the bank, and, finally, that desire won out. "Shove her in there and let's get a move on it," he finally growled.

"Okay, Jenny, I'll boost you through the window, then you can come around and unlock the door for us," Stevie instructed, taking Jenny's hand and leading her over to the window.

"I know," Jenny shot back, her tone high and mighty. She stuck out her tongue at Elmo. "I know what to do! You don't have to tell me," she allowed.

Red color shot up Elmo's neck and spread quickly across his face. "Why you little . . . ," he muttered, his hands twisting into claws and going for her throat.

"Hey, Elmo! Don't hurt her!" Lester shouted, jerking his brother back. "Least, not till she gets that door open."

Lester managed to hold his brother back until Stevie boosted Jenny through the window. In a twinkle, she wormed through the window and was opening the door. Elmo shoved her aside and rushed into the bank. He scurried across the room and over to the safe. He wrapped his arms around the lockbox, hugging the thing like it was part of the family.

"You guys really know how to open a safe?" Stevie asked, sounding like he couldn't believe it. "I always heard it was mighty hard to open one of them things."

"*Peshaw!*" Elmo snorted, backing away. "It's high time you kept your yap shut and learned a thing or two. Now, back off and give me room to work."

An amused smirk on his face, Stevie backed away. He shook his head as Elmo drew his gun and sighted carefully on the dial of the safe. "That won't work," Stevie said quietly.

His eyes blazing, Elmo whirled to face the boy. "Dad burn it, boy. You done went and loused up my aim," he said, seething.

"Doesn't matter. Them doors are too hard. The bullets will just bounce off," Stevie maintained quietly.

"Yeah, what do you know? You're just a pup," Elmo sneered and shook his fist at the boy. "Now, shut up and let me work," Elmo snapped, drawing a bead on the safe.

"Jenny, get down!" Stevie shouted, pulling his sister behind the counter and pushing her to the floor.

With a little yell, Elmo commenced to blasting. As the bullets ricocheted off the safe and screamed around the room, Lester belly-flopped down beside the two kids. Smiling, Elmo shot at the lock, jerking the trigger until the gun was empty. By then, he had bullets ricocheting around the room like a swarm of wasps.

His weapon empty, Elmo calmly stuffed it in his belt and strutted over to the safe. He shot a superior-looking smirk back over his shoulder as the others were just now venturing cautiously from cover. Elmo sniffed and rolled his shoulders, ready to have the last laugh on that bratty kid. The smirk slowly drained off his face as he tried the door and found it still locked tight.

"Shut up!" Elmo growled, stabbing a finger at Stevie before the boy had a chance to gloat. Muttering vehemently under his breath about how kids should be seen but not heard, Elmo began to slam fresh shells into his pistol. "You just wait, kid. A couple of more slugs will pry that door wide open!"

"No time for that!" Lester screamed from the front window. "Folks are pouring outta them houses like a kicked-over ant den, and they don't look happy!"

Chapter Five

By the time Elmo rushed to the window, the townsfolk of Whiskey City milled around in the middle of the street. As they looked up and down the street, trying to figure out where the shots came from, Stevie Hunt leaned against the wall of the bank and laughed. "I told you this plan wouldn't work. Now you're gonna get caught."

Elmo's face clouded up and his lower lip stuck out about a foot. "Yeah, a lot you know!" he sputtered. "I still got a trick or two up my sleeve."

Stevie laughed and nudged his sister with an elbow. "If you want to get out of this bank in one piece, you Nbest pull one of them tricks out. Them folks are gonna think to look in here mighty quick," he said tauntingly.

Elmo frowned, knowing Stevie was right and not liking it one bit. His brother, Lester, liked it even less. Lester wiped his hands on the front of his shirt and licked his lips. "Do something, Elmo," he pleaded. "I don't want to got to jail."

"I could help you," Stevie offered calmly. "But then you'd have to help me back."

"Do it, Elmo," Lester urged, sinking down till his chin rested on the windowsill. A whimper came through his lips as his eyes remained glued to the window. "I see that mean ol' Iris out there and she's totin' that buffalo gun!" he squeaked, his voice getting higher with each word.

Elmo frowned and hitched up his britches. He pulled his gun out of the holster, then shoved it back in. "Won't do no harm to hear you out," he decided, staring sourly at the two youngsters. "Well, we ain't got all night. What's your big plan?" he shouted, waving his arms over his head.

Stevie smiled smugly. "It's simple. You take us hostage. They won't give you no trouble if you threaten to hurt us."

Despite the fact that he had been ready to scoff at whatever idea Stevie came up with, Elmo liked the plan. Lester, on the other hand, was mortified by the notion. "Oh, no!" he screeched, backing away and holding his hands in front of him. "Don't listen to the little brat, he's plumb crazy," Lester howled. "You know what them folks would do to us for messing with their youngsters? Why, they'd hunt us to the end of the world, and if one of them little nubbers happens to so much as nick a fingernail . . ." Lester started shuddering at the very idea.

Stevie shook his head quickly. "You don't have to worry about that. We don't know anybody in this town. Our folks were killed and we were coming here to live with the preacher and his wife. You saw us on the stage.''

Elmo eyed the little worm warily and pulled at the scraggly growth on his chin. Elmo didn't like either one of the little sand pups, but if they could get them safely out of town, Elmo figured he could put up with them for a little while. Once they were safely out of town, he and Lester could leave the kids along the trail.

Lester's shrieking voice cut through Elmo's thoughts. ''Holy joe, they found us!'' Lester bellered, waving frantically at the window.

Elmo scurried across the bank to the front window and the sight of all those people advancing grimly at the bank made up his mind. ''Okay, kid. We'll do it your way. What do we do now?''

Stevie Hunt grinned and laid out his plan.

Almost too afraid to move, Catrinia Romanov gingerly tested the bonds around her wrists. She couldn't be sure, but they seemed a bit looser. Bending her fingers around, she worked at the knots. As she strained to loosen the knots, her eyes never left Ferrell Cauruthers.

Cauruthers sat beside the fire. He was, of all things, reading a book. Every little bit, he would look over the top of the book and stare sternly at her.

Those times, Catrinia would shrink back and hold her breath. Since they had eaten, he hadn't spoken a word, and his silence frightened her much more than his threats had.

As she pried at the knots, she wondered if he would check her bonds before he went to sleep. She remembered too well what he said he would do if she tried to escape.

When he yawned and set the book aside, Catrinia's heart skipped a beat. She knew he would check her bonds and find she had loosened them. Instead, he smiled at her. "You can quit glaring at me. It ain't gonna do you any good," he said, wry humor sounding in his voice.

"It makes me feel better," she declared.

"Suit yourself," Cauruthers replied with a shrug. He took a blanket and draped it over her shoulders. "I suggest you get some sleep. Believe me, you're gonna need it."

"Why? What are you going to do?"

"You'll find out soon enough," Cauruthers replied as he spread his own blankets on the ground. He took off his boots and slipped into his bed. With a mighty yawn, he tipped his hat over his face. "I know you're thinking of trying to make a break for it tonight, but I'm warning you, I sleep real light. You try anything and I'll hear it. Then I'll tan your backside."

"You wouldn't dare!" Catrinia flared. "I am Grand Duchess Catrinia Romanov, daughter of the czar of Russia!"

"Maybe that means something in Russia, but over here it don't mean squat."

Coldly furious, Catrinia ground her teeth and kept

quiet. She told herself that she wouldn't honor this oaf by responding to his ignorant babble. Still fuming, she waited impatiently for him to go to sleep. Finally, she was rewarded with the sound of deep snores.

Using her rage as a spur, she brought the bonds to her mouth, tearing at the knots with her teeth. The work she had done earlier with her fingers had helped, but it was still a heartbreaking struggle. Her arms ached and her teeth hurt, but this time she finally freed her hands. Once her hands were free, it didn't take but a few minutes to loosen the ropes around her feet.

Cauruthers's snoring hadn't changed pitch, so she felt sure he was still asleep, and she didn't want to wake him. Moving an inch at a time, she let the blanket fall from her shoulders and began to crawl from the camp.

Thorns tore at her clothing and scratched her face. A feeling of hopelessness and despair welled up inside Catrinia. Fighting back the tears, she crawled blindly. Her whole body shook with fear as she listened to Cauruthers's steady snoring. Any second she knew he would wake up and catch her. Catrinia did not want to think about what would happen then.

After what seemed to be hours, she was twenty yards from the camp and she felt safe to stand. Rising to her feet, she continued to edge away, fighting the urge to run.

She tried to move carefully, but she wasn't careful enough. She stepped on a branch; the resulting crack was very loud in the stillness of the night.

Cauruthers's snoring ended in a loud snort. Catrinia froze in her tracks, her ears straining and hoping against hope that he would go back to sleep. He didn't. "Hey! Come back!" he yelled.

Catrinia didn't wait to hear any more. With a little squeal, she took off running, her feet flying over the ground. Running full tilt and looking back over her shoulder, Catrinia never saw the ground drop sharply away in front of her. She never knew it until she felt herself falling. She fell a long time, the lost cry wailing into the dark night.

Chapter Six

"There's someone in the bank!" Milton Andrews, who owned the bank, shouted. His chubby face mortified at the very thought that someone might steal even one of his lovely dollars, Milt took a couple of staggering steps in the direction of the bank. "I tell you, I saw someone move in there."

The rest of the crowd exchanged amused glances. They all knew how Milt was. When it came to his money, the banker was spooked as a doe caught in a snowbank. "Isn't somebody going to do something?" he wailed, wringing his hands. "Where the devil is Teddy?"

"He's out looking for that so-called Russian princess," Louis Claude barked and spat in disgust. Mr. Claude was French and he had little use for Russians. Course, Louis didn't have much use for anything that didn't help his crops grow.

"Of all things," Andrews fumed. "I swear, I don't know about that boy. He's supposed to be guarding the town, that's his job." Andrews started to say more, but then he remembered how much he owed Teddy. With a visible effort, he swallowed the angry words that wanted desperately to get out. "What are we going to do?" he asked, his eyes scanning the crowd; then a thought occurred to him. "Bobby Stamper! Are you here, boy?"

Yawning, Bobby stepped forward. "Yeah, I'm here. I'd rather be sleeping, but I'm here."

Like a drowning man clutching a lifeline, Andrews grabbed the front of Bobby's shirt. "You used to rob banks. You know about these things. What should we do now?"

Bobby looked down at the portly banker, then to the bank, a devilish smile slowly spreading across his face. He patted Andrews on the shoulder. "Don't worry, Milt ol' boy. I know just what to do."

His face sagging with relief, Andrews clasped his hands together in front of his face. "Praise the heavens."

Bobby walked around Andrews and approached the bank nonchalantly. He stopped in the middle of the street directly in front of the bank. "You in the bank; come out with your hands in the air." He paused and winked back at Andrews. "Come out, or we'll burn the place around your ears."

"What!" Andrews screeched, nearly keeling over in the street. "You can't do that!"

A serious expression riding on his face, Bobby glanced back over his shoulder. "I'm sorry, Milt, but it's really the only way," Bobby said with a sad shake of his head. Now, Bobby might have looked sad for the banker's benefit, but when he turned back to the bank, a grin was plastered clear across his face. One thing in life that Bobby Stamper really loved was tormenting bankers. "Are you coming out, or do I have to go get the kerosene?" he called at the dark building.

Bobby didn't think for a second that there was a soul in the bank. He figured Andrews was just imagining things again. Old Milt was always conjuring up images of someone stealing his money. In his quest to have a little fun with Andrews, Bobby completely forgot about the shots that woke them all. Had he been thinking of them shots, he wouldn't have presented such a bold target.

Inside the bank, Elmo drew a bead on the center of Bobby's chest. "That's Bobby Stamper," he growled. "I never did like the polecat. I oughta grease the varmint right here and now."

"I wouldn't do that," Stevie Hunt put in quietly. "You kill one of their friends and they'll never let you out of town alive."

Elmo knew the little toad jumper was right, but he couldn't help but think what it would be like if he shot. The man that finally downed Bobby Stamper! Wow! Why, he'd be famous!

Elmo became so engrossed with the thought that he almost squeezed the trigger. The thing that stopped him was the thought of all them guns out there. He wouldn't live long enough to enjoy his newfound fame. Still, it was an intriguing thought.

As Elmo came out of his dreams, he heard Bobby call once again for them to give up. This time Stamper backed up his threats by lighting a match and holding it over his head.

The sight of that cocky devil Stamper sent a jet of rage through Elmo. "I reckon it's time to show them folks we mean business," he growled. Lifting his rifle again, he sighted down the barrel and pulled the trigger.

Bobby was watching the flame on the end of the match die when the shot sounded. At the sound of the shot, Bobby threw himself backward, slipping and plowing into the ground. Scrambling on his hands and knees, he scooted across the street. He was all the way across the street, crouched behind a water trough, before he realized the shot hadn't been fired at him, but at the ground between his legs. "Sweet Molly Brown, there's somebody in there!" Bobby exclaimed.

Inside the bank, Elmo hooted gleefully. "Did you see that stuffed shirt tuck tail and run?" he chortled. "I bet it'll be a week 'fore his backside unpuckers."

The once crammed street was now eerily empty as the citizens of Whiskey City took cover where they could find it. Burdett, the blacksmith, cowered behind the water trough with Bobby. Half out of breath, the big smith looked across to Bobby. "Are you hurt, boy?"

Bobby grinned and shook his head. "Nothing but my pride, Sam," he replied cheerfully.

"Well, I'm glad you're okay," Burdett said with a grunt. "I think I pulled a muscle in my leg. Darn leg's been giving me trouble for weeks. Reckon it's gout. Went to see that new doc over in Central City, but he . . .''

As Burdett rambled on, Bobby began to wish he'd stayed out in the street and slugged it out with the outlaws. Likely, he woulda been shot, maybe even killed, but that couldn't be worse than being trapped here and having to listen to Burdett.

Finally, Bobby had all he could take. "Excuse me, Sam, but I best see if I can talk to these fellers," Bobby put in when Burdett paused for a breath. Before the smith could protest, Bobby raised his head cautiously above the trough. "You in the bank," he called out softly, "we got you surrounded and we're giving you one chance to give yourselves up."

Inside the bank, Lester backed away from the window, nervously fingering his gun. "I dunno, Elmo, there's a pile of them out there. Maybe we should do like he said and give up."

"Aw, be quiet, Lester," Elmo growled.

Scolded, Lester slunk over to the middle of the room, throwing himself down on the floor beside little Jenny Hunt. She looked up at him with big round eyes. "Are you scared, Lester?" she asked.

"Yes, I am," Lester said defiantly. "Ain't you scared?" he asked, watching as young Stevie and Elmo held a powwow.

Her eyes sparkling, Jenny shook her head. "Oh, no. This is fun!"

As they talked, Stevie came over and knelt beside them. He nodded to Elmo, who broke the window with his rifle. "You folks best hold your fire. We got hostages," he yelled through the hole in the glass.

"Elmo, is that you?" Bobby called back, with genuine fondness in his voice. "Who's your hostage? Lester?" he asked gleefully.

"Not hardly," Elmo grumped. "Cock your ears open and take a listen to this!"

Stevie placed his hand on his sister's shoulder. "Okay, Jenny, give us one of your best screams."

Jenny sucked in a deep breath and let out a scream that woulda put a train whistle to shame. Stevie had known what was coming and covered his ears. Not so with poor Lester.

As the scream died away, Lester surged to his feet, clapping his hands over his ears. "Lordy, I'm deaf!" he screeched. Stagging in circles, he banged into a desk knocking a lamp off. The lamp shattered on the floor with a loud crash.

"Be quiet," Elmo hissed at his brother, then hollered out the window. "Now, you know we got a couple of kids in here. You do what we say, or you'll be having a couple of kiddie-sized funerals."

Outside, Milton Andrews scurried over to the trough. "I heard something break! What did they break?" he wheezed.

"A window and something else, sounded like a lamp," Bobby said absently as he tried to think. "All right, Elmo, what do you want?" he called.

"We don't want nothing but to get outta town," Elmo shouted in return. A sour expression on his face, Elmo shot a scowl at Stevie. "I still think we should make that fat boy banker come over here and pry that safe open for us."

"You take the money and they'll not be so ready to let you leave town," Stevie reminded him. "Besides, I got something else in mind."

Outside, Milt grabbed the front of Bobby's shirt, drawing him close. "You're not actually thinking of letting them just ride out of town?" he demanded.

"Not much else we can do," Bobby said with a shrug. "That sounded like little Jenny Hunt. I reckon they got her and Stevie in there."

Andrews frowned, releasing Bobby's shirt. "Them the kids that came into town with Preacher Tom's wife?" he asked, rubbing his chin.

"Yeah," Bobby replied, looking at the men around him. "We best do what they say. Now, I know Elmo and Lester are harmless, but they're also foul-ups. They're liable to hurt them kids by accident."

Andrews frowned even deeper. "Don't get me wrong," he said slowly. "I'm worried about them kids same as you, but there's no need to be hasty. We oughta think this over for a spell before we just let them waltz outta town."

"Relax, Milt. I could hear them talking. They didn't get into the safe," Bobby explained patiently.

"Well, that's different then," Milt said quickly. All

of a sudden he got all generous. "I reckon it's the safety of them kids we should be considering."

As his words died away, a loud crash sounded from inside the bank. Burdett smiled and whacked Andrews across the back. "Reckon that was that fancy spittoon you keep on your desk," he said gravely.

"My Chinese vase," Milt whispered. "For pete's sake, let's give them what they want and get them outta there before they wreck the place," he pleaded desperately.

"Whatever you say," Bobby grunted, then stood up. "Okay, Elmo. Tell us what you want to do."

They had to wait as they heard a lot of arguing from inside. Finally Elmo called out. "All we want is a couple of saddle horses brought around back. Just to make sure you don't foller us, we'll take the kids aways out of town, then leave them."

Bobby frowned, he didn't like that. "All right, Elmo, you're calling the shots," he agreed (he had little choice). "But if them kids get hurt, you'll wish you never been born."

Inside, Elmo kicked his toe against the wall and grumbled. "That dang Stamper. He still thinks he's running this here show. I shoulda smoked the stuffed shirt when I had the chance," he fumed, prowling the room. With a sweep of his rifle, he knocked a lamp off its wall mount. Even before the sound of the crash died away, they heard a shriek of anguish from outside.

Little Jenny climbed to her feet, tugging on Elmo's

shirttail. "How come you don't like Bobby?" she asked innocently. "I think he's nice. He bought some candy for me one time."

"I just don't like him, that's all," Elmo muttered, which wasn't quite true. It wasn't so much that Elmo didn't like Bobby, but that he was jealous of him. Bobby was everything Elmo wanted to be and couldn't quite pull off. Mad again, Elmo broke another lamp.

Out in the street, Andrews was blubbering like a kid with a mashed thumb. "We got to get them out of there," the banker moaned. "I just spent a fortune rebuilding the place, and now they are wrecking it."

"Somebody slap a muzzle on him," Iris Stevens barked. She marched up to them carrying a big Sharps fifty. "Am I to understand that the two men holed up in the bank are the same ones who kidnapped me last fall?"

"Yeah, that's them all right," Bobby admitted, watching the old gal like a hawk. "This ain't the time to be thinking of settling a grudge, Iris," he warned.

" 'Course it ain't!" she snapped, grounding the butt of that big gun down on his toe. "But if one of them happens to walk in front of my rifle, I reckon I'd be obligated to yank the trigger."

Bobby grimaced, partly from the stabbing pain in his foot and partly just because Iris was around. He wouldn't give her the satisfaction of grabbing his toe. "Now, Iris, that's the kind of talk that's gonna get one of them kids killed. Why don't you just go home and let us handle this."

"Yeah? Well, what knucklehead went and put you in charge?"

"Nobody," Bobby admitted, his voice tight as he tried to keep his temper in check. "I'm just trying to keep them kids from getting killed. Now, why don't you butt out and go home?"

Iris's face turned red as she spit and sputtered. "Butt out, you say!" she roared. "You can't talk to me that-away!"

"I can and I did," Bobby snapped back. "Now leave us alone."

For a minute, Iris stormed and put up a balky front, but she gave up without much of a scrap. Dragging that big rifle behind her, she shuffled off to her house.

Looking back on it, Bobby knew he shouldn't have trusted her meekness. That woman didn't have a meek bone in her whole leathery body. Iris Stevens had been born mean, and gotten better at it as the years went by. Bobby knew all of this, but at the time he was busy and just glad to see her go.

As Iris disappeared into her house, Mr. Burdett and Mr. Claude led two saddle horses up from Burdett's livery stable. "Go ahead and lead them around back," Bobby told the two older men. As they went around the corner of the bank, Bobby called to the men inside. "Okay, Elmo, your hosses are around back."

"We see 'em," Elmo shot back, sounding irritated. "Tell them jaspers to leave the horses in the alley, then the lot of you clear out. We don't want to see anybody when we come out."

"Okay, we're pulling back," Bobby grumbled as the people of Whiskey City slowly eased back down the street. Milt Andrews moved the slowest, holding a handkerchief to his face and grieving like a widow. One by one, they backed into the saloon. Joe Havens rushed behind the bar, ready to start pouring the drinks, but for once, nobody in Whiskey City felt like a belt.

As a group, they crowded to the windows. They pressed their noses to the yellowed glass and strained to see what was happening. As the seconds crawled by, the group became restless.

"What the devil are they doing?" Claude griped.

"They're trying to open the safe!" Andrews exclaimed. "We have to stop them!"

"Relax," Bobby replied easily. "That's a Harper-Evans safe. They'll not get it open."

"You did," Andrews grumbled sourly.

"But I'm the best," Bobby replied, a smug look on his face.

"Cocky cuss, ain't he?" Joe Havens grunted.

"Never mind that," Burdett shouted from the back door. "I can see somebody slinking around in the alley. I reckon they're getting ready to pull out."

They were in fact ready to move out. Lester was leading the way out the back door. He had just pawed out the door and into the darkness with one foot, when he ran bellyfirst into something very hard.

A grunt blowing past his lips, Lester stopped dead still. In less than a second, he began to march backward, a rifle buried in the pit of his stomach. Behind that rifle was Iris Stevens and she wasn't happy. Poking and gouging, she marched Lester backward. "Not so fast, buster," she barked. "You ain't getting away that easy."

"Elmo, help me!" Lester howled, when his back hit the counter and he could retreat no farther.

Elmo wasn't in any shape to offer assistance. He simply stood in the middle of the room, his jaw hanging down to his belt buckle.

"I've been waiting a long time to get my hands on you two no-accounts," Iris said, and she smiled, but it wasn't a comforting smile.

"Somebody help me, the old bat's gone plumb loco," Lester wailed from behind the rifle.

Stevie Hunt started to say something, but Elmo finally regained his composure and pushed the youngster aside. "I'll handle this, sonny boy," he allowed, hitching up his belt and sniffing loudly. "All right, you old battle-ax, put down that gun or I'll shoot one of these kids."

Iris shot him a hard-boiled look that was in no way impressed. She knew these two and knew they were all hot air. "I don't think you will. I could shoot your brother. I might just shoot the both of you. Lord knows I got a reason."

Elmo was a might shaken. He'd gotten used to the notion of folks backing off when he threatened to shoot one of the kids. Iris was being contrary, though. To tell the truth, she scared the bejeebers outta Elmo.

Elmo was ready to fold his deck, when Stevie whispered something in his ear. A slow smile on his face, Elmo grabbed his suspenders with both hands and puffed out his chest. "You might have a reason, but you ain't got enough bullets. That there is a single-shot shootin' iron. You might shoot Lester, but then you'll be empty."

"What?" Lester shrieked, his knees threatening to buckle. "You ain't gonna let that old bat shoot me!"

"Who you calling an old bat?" Iris shot back, doing her best to drive the barrel of that rifle right through Lester's guts.

"I'm sorry! I never meant it. Please don't shoot," Lester begged.

"She won't shoot," Elmo predicted. "She ain't got enough bullets to snuff us both. She's just bluffin'."

For an answer, Iris whirled and planted the rifle in Elmo's midsection. "You still think I'm just bluffing?"

The gulping sound from Elmo's throat could be heard clear across the room as he tried to swallow the sudden knot in his throat. "No, ma'am, I don't reckon you are," he said meekly, the gun trickling from his fingers.

"Well, if I was you I wouldn't give me a reason to shoot you, 'cause I'm dying to do it," Iris said. "Now, both of you throw down the rest of them guns."

Both Elmo and Lester got rid of their guns like the weapons was red-hot. "Ma'am, I didn't mean it when I called you an old battle-ax," Elmo said, then tried again to swallow. "You're a real purty lady."

"Yeah, right nice," Lester agreed hastily.

"Bull puckey," Iris snapped. "Ain't no use groveling. You ain't about to pull the wool over my eyes."

Stevie Hunt was amazed. He couldn't believe Lester and Elmo had given up so easily. The old woman only had one bullet, but that wasn't it. Women, especially older women, were easy to handle in Stevie's eyes. Stevie had felt sure he could handle her. All you had to do was hug them and cry a little, and women would cave right in. Stevie shook his head. If Lester and Elmo had just hung in there a minute longer, he would have talked the old woman out of her gun. That's what you get for dealing with amateurs, Stevie thought. He was working on a new plan, when Iris ordered Lester and Elmo to march.

"Yes, ma'am," they both said and threw their hands in the air and scrambled for the door. The problem was, they were in too much of a hurry to please, and tangled their feet.

They both tripped and plowed headfirst into Iris. Their combined weight was more than enough to bowl her over. With a shriek, she landed flat on her back, her feet flying up in the air and Lester and Elmo piling on top of her.

Stevie snatched the fallen rifle off the floor, having a hard time keeping both ends off the ground at the same time. "Let's go!" he shouted.

Neither Lester nor Elmo was in the mood to waste around to see if Iris was okay. Scooping up their guns, they bolted for the back door, with Stevie and Jenny right behind them. Stevie didn't like the weight of Iris's rifle, so he threw it into the shadows, then jumped on his horse. Together, the four of them rode out of town like the devil was after them.

Chapter Seven

As the first rays of the sun caught Lester and Elmo, they were a good distance from Whiskey City. They were far enough away that they were starting to breathe easier.

A sour taste in his mouth, Elmo looked over at the two little kids riding alongside them. He saw no signs of pursuit from Whiskey City, and decided this was as good a time as any to unload them kids.

Just making the decision made Elmo feel better. He frowned and shot a glance over at Stevie Hunt. Something about the brash little pup rubbed Elmo's fur the wrong way. The boy was just too cocky. The worst of it was, Stevie's plan to get them out of Whiskey City had worked. Elmo hated to admit it, but the little weasel's plan had worked slicker than slime on a frozen pond.

Just the thought of it was enough to send bolts of rage racing through Elmo's veins. Elmo jerked his horse around to face the two brats. "Okay, this is as far as you go," he snarled.

He expected the two kids to cringe back in fear, but Jenny giggled and Stevie merely stared back, like he had been expecting this. "I helped you, now it's your turn to help me," Stevie reminded.

"Fat chance, kid," Elmo replied, laughing as he thumbed his nose at the little punk.

Stevie Hunt waited until Elmo and Lester had ridden a few yards, then called out after them. "It could mean a lot of money for you."

Elmo's back stiffened like he'd been shot from behind with an arrow. "How much money?" he called back over his shoulder, his voice straining to sound casual.

Stevie smiled and shrugged. "I don't rightly know, but it'd be a lot."

Elmo looked to his brother, who was too busy eating a piece of jerky to answer. "Well, I don't reckon it would hurt to hear him out," Elmo grumbled. He spun his horse around, making a gesture for Stevie to continue. "Well, spit it out, kid. We're busy men. We ain't got time to fool around."

"You know who was on that stage you tried to rob?" Stevie asked.

"No. Who?" Elmo sneered.

"A Russian princess!" Stevie said, and despite himself, a knot of excitement crept into his voice. "After we outran you fellas, three other men jumped us. They shot the driver and another man, then took the princess away."

"That's real interesting," Elmo said, rolling his eyes

in disgust. "But I don't see how we could make any money out of it."

"What would you say if I told you that I heard them talking, and I heard them say where they was going to keep that princess."

"You think we could go and take her away from them?" Elmo asked, jerking at his ear as he thought it over.

"Let's do it, Elmo!" Lester sputtered, his cheeks packed with jerky. "I never seen a real honest-to-goodness princess before."

"She's real pretty," Jenny Hunt said. "And nice too. I liked her."

"Really? You saw her? Did she have a crown and everything?" Lester asked eagerly.

"Shut up!" Elmo snapped, silencing the pair with a sweep of his arm. He looked at Stevie and slowly shook his head. "I don't know. Three of them, that's kinda long odds. They might be tough to handle."

"No, there's just one. I heard them talking. They was gonna split up. One man was gonna take the princess up to this place in the edge of the mountains."

"You figure we could snatch this princess and hold her for ransom ourselves," Elmo suggested slyly.

"That was my plan. We could split the money fifty-fifty," Stevie said, holding out his hand gravely. "How about it? Are we partners?"

Elmo took the little hand in his own and shook it firmly. "I reckon we are," he said, licking his lips greedily. Already, Elmo was trying to figure out a way to cheat the snooty little pip-squeak out of his share.

Arkady Rostov was like a caged bear, growling and pacing while we waited for the sun to come up. Now, I was all for catching a catnap, but with Rostov on the prod, a dead man woulda had trouble sleeping.

Finally the sun did come up and light slowly spread across the land. We picked up the trail without any trouble, setting out scooting right along.

Rostov surprised me some. I'd always thought of Russians as plodding farmers, and just looking at Rostov, he seemed to fit the bill. 'Course, when he crawled up on a horse, it was a different story. He could really ride and even track a mite. When I commented on it, the Russian shot me a glance that coulda put a skim of ice on the face of the sun.

"I am a Cuisak," he replied haughtily.

Now, I had no earthly idea what a Cuisak was, but whatever Arkady Rostov was, he could ride a horse like he was part of the hair. And while he wasn't as good a tracker as me, he could follow a trail.

From the getgo, the gents who hit the stage—there were three of them—took pains to hide their trail. And believe me, they done a mighty good job of it too. That worried me. Unless they slacked up some, we were in for a devil of a time.

They had a fair jump on us and we weren't closing the gap. Then they up and done the thing I had been dreading. They split up. Now, completely hiding the tracks of four horses was a dang near impossible chore, but covering the tracks of two was a sight easier.

At the spot where they parted company, me and Rostov dismounted. Two riders had kept heading west, while the other two cut off to the south. We pored over the ground, trying to decide which way they had taken the princess.

Finally, I straightened up, pretty certain I had it figured out. "One of them took your princess and headed west, into the mountains. The other two went south. I don't know where they might be headed," I informed Rostov.

Arkady Rostov rubbed his massive chin and stared at me with a haunted expression. "You are sure?" he asked doubtfully. "Why would they take the princess into the mountains. Fort Laramie is south, no?"

"Yeah south and east of here," I answered, wondering what Laramie had to do with this.

Rostov made up his mind. I could tell by the way he set his jaw firm. "I find it easier to believe that Catrinia is one of the riders going south. Why would they want to take her up into the mountains?"

"I don't know," I admitted. "Why would they want to take her at all?"

Rostov shrugged, avoiding my question. "That is of no consequence." He hesitated, then set his jaw firm. "I am certain she went to the south. That is the way I go."

Now, I got the distinct feeling that big Russian knew a whole heap more than he was telling. "What makes you so sure of that?'' I asked. Rostov didn't seem of a mind to answer, so I pressed my point. ''If you know something you ain't telling me, you best spit it out. If we figure on rescuing your princess, we best figure out what the hombres that took her are up to. Then maybe we can get one jump ahead of them.''

For a minute, I thought Rostov would break down and spill the story, but he never done it. Instead, he clamped his mouth shut and pointed a hairy arm to the south. ''We will follow this trail.''

With that said, the stubborn cuss took off. I watched him go, and believe me, I was in a quandary. On the one hand, I was pretty certain the princess had been led away into the mountains. 'Course, I could be wrong, and if we chose the wrong trail, we might never find her.

With a sigh, I urged my horse forward, taking after Rostov. In a way, I was glad that Rostov took the decision out of my hands. I knew if I guessed wrong and something happened to that princess, I'd never be able to live with myself. Still, I knew we were chasing down the wrong trail and that didn't set right.

I caught up with that Russian and by then, I was determined to see if I could bore some sense into that thick skull of his. 'Course, with a granite noggin like his, I knew it would take some doing.

''Look, Arkady,'' I started, trying to keep it friendly. ''If you ask me, I'd say we are follering the wrong trail.''

Rostov turned in the saddle, laying a pair of ice-cold eyes on me. ''I did not ask you,'' he replied stiffly. He pulled himself up straight in the saddle. "I am not in the habit of asking common rubes for their opinion."

Why of all the persnickety things! Why, I had a good notion to jar his snoot with my fist. I thought about it and believe me, I dearly wanted to do 'er, but somehow I held back. We were out here to save the life of a young lady and I was doing my level best to remember that. "Look, I may be a rube, but at least I ain't the one heading off in the wrong direction while some cutthroat hightails it the other way with my princess."

For a response, Rostov only grunted and kept right on riding. Gritting my teeth, I pounded my fist into my thigh. I swear, that Russian was as hardheaded as a stove-up mule. "If you would take the time to notice, you'd see that these two hombres is riding side by side. The other trail, the horses was single file, like one of them was being led."

Now, I don't know if I was getting to him or just getting under his skin, but either way, he lifted his horse into a trot and rode away from me. I glared at his broad back, cussin' under my breath. Dang fool was gonna lose the trail hauling along like he was. Then I realized he wouldn't. The trail was now as plain as a skirt on a sow. When I caught up to him and pointed out that little fact, he looked at me, and for the first time, I could see doubt in his eyes.

He rode in silence for a ways, then shook his head. "No matter, I ride this way," he said, grunting.

I groaned and cussed some more. I was just hunting myself a new way to come at him, when I saw it. Just a lump lying in the trail, but it looked out of place.

Even though we were a good ways off, I recognized the heap for what it was. There's something about the body of a man that stands out. And that's what this was, a dead man sprawled across the trail.

Two hours after sunup, Bobby Stamper and Mr. Claude rode back into Whiskey City. They rode dejected, their heads down. Last night, they had gone out to pick up Stevie and Jenny Hunt and hadn't found the youngsters.

Both men were hoarse from shouting and feeling low. Bobby cursed himself for not getting on the trail sooner. After Lester and Elmo left town, the whole bunch of them had rushed down to the bank, hoping the two brothers had been bluffing and left the kids behind.

They didn't find the kids, but what they did find was Iris stretched out cold on the floor. After they roused the old gal, they had to endure five minutes of ranting and raving before she spit out her story.

It took her a while to tell it too. She had to stop every little bit and froth about what she was going to do to Lester and Elmo if she ever got her hands on them.

By the time she finished, Lester and Elmo had a good lead. A lead that stretched as Bobby and Louis Claude saddled their horses. It was too dark to track, so Bobby and Louis simply rode out in the same direction, calling Stevie and Jenny's names.

At dawn, they still hadn't found the youngsters and began looking for tracks. Two hours later, they gave up and rode back into town.

Burdett was at his shop when they rode in. "Them kids show up yet?" Claude asked.

Hammer in hand, Burdett stared back at them and shook his head. "You didn't find them?"

"No," Bobby answered, swinging down. "We best get some supplies together and go looking for them."

A worried frown on his face, Burdett took a long step back. "I'd sure like to go along, but I got a turrible crick in my neck. Can't hardly move my head at all. Don't reckon I'd be much help," he said, looking hopefully at the two men. "Besides, I reckon somebody ought to stay here in case they wander in on their own."

Neither Bobby nor Louis followed the logic behind that, but they knew from experience that making Burdett do something was more trouble than it was worth. They were just leaving the stable when two men rode in.

They were big men, dressed in plain black coats and wearing still, watchful expressions. Bobby paused, watching them closely. Had they been wearing pistols, Bobby would have said they were gunmen. But aside from their rifles in the saddleboots, they carried no visible weapons. Curious, Bobby turned back and heard them ask, in thick accents, about putting their horses up.

"Sure thing," Burdett agreed, stroking the neck of one of the animals. "What brings you boys into Whiskey City?"

"We came to see Grand Duchess Catrinia," the older of the pair announced, passing his reins to Burdett.

"You boys are from Russia, then?" Bobby asked, studying them. They were both as tall as Bobby, with slightly bigger builds. Bobby judged the elder to be in his forties, the other ten years younger. They both looked fit and ready, and Bobby couldn't shake the feeling that they were fighting men.

Again, it was the older man who answered. "Yes. We emigrated to this country two years ago. When we heard the duchess would be stopping here, we had to come. We miss hearing our native language, and we wished to hear news of the old country."

"And to see Catrinia. Just to see such a lady is an honor. We hope to speak with her, which would indeed be a privilege."

"You may not get the chance," Claude told them. "We have reason to believe that she has been kidnapped."

The two Russians exchanged quick glances, but they showed no signs of emotion. "That is terrible news. Is there anything we can do to help?" the young one offered.

"We got men on it," Bobby replied. " 'Bout all we can do now is wait."

"In that case, could you direct us to the hotel?" the older man asked.

Bobby pointed out the hotel and watched as they slowly walked to it. Something about those two bothered him. He couldn't put his finger on it, but there was something.

"Bobby, if we are going after them kids, we best get some supplies and go," Louey called.

"Yeah," Bobby said and grunted, watching as the two Russians entered the hotel.

The two men registered, then went quickly up to their room. It was only after they were inside that they showed emotion. The younger man looked to his older companion and smiled. "So, Dmitri," he said. "I see Boris Fedarov has been busy."

Dmitri allowed himself the tiniest of smiles and nodded. "So it would seem, Vanya." Dmitri walked to the window and looked out, watching as Bobby and Louis rode out of town. "Just think, Vanya. In a few days, this will all be over. They shall all be dead and we shall be in power."

Vanya took a bottle of vodka from the saddlebag he carried and poured some into two glasses from the nightstand. "To a new Russia!" he said, holding out the glasses.

Chapter Eight

Catrinia Romanov woke slowly. At first, she had trouble orientating herself, as a dull ache pounded at her head. She felt something damp and cool on her head. She could hear the gentle murmur of a soft voice, but couldn't quite make out the words. She felt the coolness leave her head, then return. Catrinia let out a sigh, it felt so good to simply lie here.

How tired she was. For a second, Catrinia was ready to slip back into the gentle embrace of sleep, but then she remembered. She remembered the swift attack on the stage, but mostly she remembered Ferrell Cauruthers and his cold threats. She had to get out of here before he found her!

With a start, Catrinia tried to sit up. The sudden movement sent an avalanche of pain shooting through her head. With a low groan, she collapsed back.

"Don't try to move," a voice said, then she saw the face of Ferrell Cauruthers loom over her.

A little bleat of fear escaped past her lips as she shrank back into her blankets. Cauruthers mistook her whimper as one of pain. With gentle fingers, he took the damp cloth from her forehead and rinsed it with water from his canteen. "I know it hurts," he said softly as he placed the cool rag back on her head. "You got a nasty bump on your head. There ain't a lot I can do for it."

"Isn't," Catrinia whispered. "It is correct to say, there *isn't* a lot you can do."

Cauruthers smiled weakly. "I reckon you're right about that," he acknowledged and pulled the blanket up tighter around her. "You just lie still and get some rest." He leaned back, wringing his hands and looking around. "Are you cold? I could start a fire."

Catrinia nodded absently, feeling sleep slowly overtake her. She watched groggily as Cauruthers put together the fire. As the glow of the flames spread a warmth over her, she fell asleep.

When Catrinia again woke, it was broad daylight and the fire had burned down to nothing. Ferrell Cauruthers sat beside her, his arms wrapped around his body as he slept. He shivered in his sleep and she wondered where his coat was. She soon discovered that he had given her both blankets and used his jacket to make a pillow for her.

Even though her head ached dully, Catrinia Romanov smiled. It had been quite cold last night, but Cauruthers had given his coat to her. She remembered his gentle touch as he tried to care for her, and she no longer feared Ferrell Cauruthers.

Without thinking, she reached out and touched his

hand lightly. He came awake with a bang, startling her. She noticed that his first reaction was to grab the butt of his gun and look all around him quickly.

Seeing no danger, he relaxed quickly and easily, even smiling down at her. "How are you feeling this morning, ma'am?" he asked with real concern in his voice.

"My head hurts, but otherwise I feel fine," Catrinia answered. "I would appreciate it if you would be so kind as to escort me into Whiskey City."

"Fat chance," Cauruthers muttered, his eyes wandering off into the distance. "What I ought to do is fan your backside with a hemp rope for trying to escape."

Last night, that threat would have frightened Catrinia, but not this morning. She thought she knew Cauruthers. Despite the pain in her head, she smiled up at him. "You won't do that," she replied smugly. "I saw how you took care of me last night. You wouldn't hurt me."

"Don't bet on it, lady," Cauruthers growled, trying to scowl down at her and not quite pulling it off. "I'm a mighty mean man, and you'd be well advised not to forget it."

Clutching the blankets to her, Catrinia sat up and pulled his coat from underneath her. She held it up for him to see, then passed the coat to him. "You gave up your jacket for me. Face it, Mr. Cauruthers, you're a kind and thoughtful man. A gentleman."

Cauruthers snorted and snatched the jacket from her. "I been called a lot of things, but kind ain't one of them," he growled as he shrugged into the coat.

Catrinia laughed, a light delicate sound. She laughed with ease and warmth, like someone who laughed a lot. As her laughter died away, she put a mock-serious look on her face and pointed a slender finger at Cauruthers. "You do not fool me, sir. You're an honorable man at heart. You cannot hope to hide that, not now. Your actions last night gave you away. Now, I would be most grateful if you would escort me into Whiskey City where I might rejoin my friends."

Cauruthers swore vehemently under his breath. He cursed Catrinia for seeing deeper into him than he liked. He cursed his partner, Bill Paulson, for talking him into this crazy scheme. Mostly, he cursed himself for not doing a better job of tying her last night.

It had occurred to him to tie her hands behind her back, but last night he hadn't seen the need. She'd acted so scared and meek that he never dreamed she would give him any trouble. To tell the truth, he'd felt sorry for her. Even though he'd thought about tying her hands behind her back, he'd never done it. Knowing she'd be more comfortable, he'd simply tied her hands loosely in front of her. And how did she repay him? She'd went and escaped. Cauruthers grumbled to himself. It never failed, you tried to be nice to someone and they shafted you.

"Mr. Cauruthers, all that grunting and swearing isn't doing anybody any good, and quite frankly, I find it most offensive."

For a second, Catrinia thought she had pushed him too

far. Anger blazing in his eyes, he swore again. As she shrank back and pulled the blanket up tighter under her chin, the anger drained from his face, replaced by a look of guilt. "Sorry, ma'am," he mumbled.

Catrinia sat up, her expression stiffly dignified and her tone high and mighty. "Could you please take me into Whiskey City. I want to see my friends."

"Lady, you ain't in charge here," Ferrell grunted, then slid a glance at her out of the corner of his eye. "Besides, what makes you so sure you have friends there?" Cauruthers asked slyly.

"Of course," Catrinia replied. She started to dismiss Cauruthers's remark, but something in his face stopped her. He was too smug. He knew something. "What about my friends?"

"You don't have any friends," Ferrell Cauruthers gloated. He was being cruel and he knew it, but he was upset with her and he reckoned she deserved it. "You ever stop to think about what happened to all them fellers that was supposed to be guarding you?"

"Arkady went ahead to make sure all the preparations were being made. The rest of the men were sick, and Boris stayed behind to attend to some business."

Ferrell Cauruthers laughed. "Your Boris had business, all right. He was busy paying me and my partner to snatch you off the stage. As for the others, they weren't sick, that Boris feller bought them off."

Catrinia was shocked and she showed it. "You're lying!" she snapped, paying no attention to the pain as she tossed her head. "I've known Boris Fedarov for years. His family has being serving mine for generations."

"Yeah, well maybe he got tired of fetchin' and carryin' for a spoiled snob like you," Ferrell shot back.

Catrinia's face flamed bright red as her royal blood boiled. "Maybe you do not know the meaning of honor and loyalty, but there are those who do. Boris Fedarov has served my family valiantly. His loyalty is above question!" Even as she spoke, Catrinia didn't really believe what she was saying. She had never liked nor trusted Fedarov.

Cauruthers snorted and slapped his leg. "That Fedarov is a weasel if I ever saw one. The only thing he is loyal to is himself."

"And yet you help him?" Catrinia accused, already believing the worst about Fedarov. Her words hit a nerve with Cauruthers, she could tell from the way he hurriedly ducked his head and put all his attention into building a fire.

"He pays good and I needed the money," Cauruthers answered after a lengthy pause. He knew he'd be better off keeping quiet, but for some reason, he felt the need to explain things to her. "He said you weren't to be hurt, he just wanted to use you to get your family out of power. He described your kind as cruel and vindictive people who ruled their land with an iron fist."

"And you believed him?" she asked quietly.

"No, I don't reckon," Ferrell muttered, his head still down. "But he was paying top dollar and my partner was going along, so I up and did it."

"Do you still think my people are cruel and vindictive?" Catrinia asked, and Cauruthers shook his head. "Then why do you continue to hold me prisoner, helping such a man as Boris Fedarov?"

Surprise showed on Cauruthers's face, as he looked at her. "I gave my word, ma'am."

Coldly furious, Catrinia tried to think. It surprised her that she believed Ferrell Cauruthers, but she did. Of course, she had never liked Fedarov.

Catrinia knew now why Arkady Rostov had been sent ahead, which was not his usual task. Arkady would have never allowed this to happen. She knew Arkady loved her like she was one of his own children, as did Nikolai. Nikolai! He'd been on the stage with her.

A feeling of dread swept through her and a tear fell from her eye. "What happened to Nikolai?" she whispered, already knowing the answer. Cauruthers didn't answer, he merely raised an eyebrow and shrugged. "Nikolai! The man who accompanied me on the stage. What happened to him?" she demanded fiercely.

Ferrell Cauruthers looked at his boots for a long time, then finally met her gaze. "He's dead, ma'am," he replied quietly.

For a full second, Catrinia Romanov sat in stunned silence, feeling like a ton of bricks just fell on her. Poor Nikolai. She remembered vividly the day Nikolai taught her to ride. Since her earliest memory, Nikolai had been at her side, offering protection, teaching her. Catrinia buried her face in her hands and cried.

Ferrell Cauruthers rose to his feet and smoothed his jeans with his hands. He looked at the mountains rising up in the west and chewed his lip. Finally, he moved stiffly to the princess's side and put his arm awkwardly around her shoulder. "I'm terribly sorry, ma'am," he said, his voice husky.

Catrinia raised her head, her eyes flashing daggers. "I just bet you are. You killed him!" she flared, beating his chest and arms with her tiny fists.

Cauruthers fell back under her furious assault. "No, ma'am, I never done it!" he screeched desperately as he tried to protect himself. "It was one of your Russian pals."

Catrinia stopped in midswing, staring down at him. "What do you mean?" she asked as she wiped the tears from her cheeks.

"You don't remember?" Cauruthers asked.

Catrinia shook her head slowly, knowing he meant the stage holdup. "It all happened so fast," she wailed. "We were sitting in the stage while the driver checked the team. I heard some shots, then Nikolai jumped from the stage. I remember the stage took off wildly, and the next thing I knew I woke up in your camp."

Cauruthers sat down beside her. He knew he shouldn't tell her anything, but all of a sudden, he wanted her to know that he wasn't the one that killed that Nikolai feller. "We came up on the stage from the west and found it stopped, with the driver out tending to the hosses," he began, rolling a cigarette as he talked. "Me

and Bill—that's my partner—we figured to slip down
and take everybody by surprise. We hadn't planned on
hurting anyone, but like I said, we had one of your Russian guards with us. I don't reckon ol' Boris trusted us,
so he sent this Russian jasper along. That Russian, he
opened fire on the driver, then when that Nikolai came
boiling out of the stage, he shot him too.''

"Which one of my guards was with you?"

"He said his name was Yakov. Don't know whether
that's first or last.''

Catrinia shuddered as she remembered Yakov. He was
one of the new men that Boris Fedarov had hired. A
small dark man, Yakov had an enormous temper and an
ogling stare. She remembered the way he kept bumping
into her and felt her skin crawl. "What's going to happen
to me now?" she asked, fighting back the tears.

Once again, Cauruthers looked away, clearing his
throat several times. "I don't rightly know. I was told to
bring you here and hold you. Yakov headed back to Fort
Laramie to tell Fedarov we had you. My partner Bill
Paulson went to get some supplies.''

As Ferrell finished, he could tell she was crying again.
He took off his hat, mumbling miserably under his
breath. To tell the truth, Ferrell Cauruthers felt lower
than a boot heel. Right then, he almost wished she was
mad again. Even that screaming and hitting would be
easier to take than all this crying.

Now, Ferrell Cauruthers had heard the old saying, be
careful what you wish for, 'cause you just might get it.

Oh yeah, he'd heard it, but he never paid it any mind. And he was going to regret that.

Tears streaming down her face, Catrinia looked down at her white hands resting in her lap. Nothing in her sheltered, protected life had prepared her for this. The blanket had slipped off her shoulders, and she started to pull it up, when her hands froze. Her eyes snapping wide open with shock, she stared down at the buttons on her dress, which had been loosened. Screeching Russian curses, she snatched up a stick and began to pummel the unsuspecting Cauruthers.

She drove the big gunman back as she screamed at him, comparing his ancestry to that of a jackass. The stick shattered in her hands and she threw it aside. She jumped at Cauruthers, her fingernails going for his eyes. He cried out in pain as they dug into the soft flesh of his cheek.

Ferrell Cauruthers was a strong young man and right then a mighty mad one. With a tremendous roar, he threw her off. Blood streaming down his cheeks and his face wild with pain and anger, Ferrell Cauruthers's hand swooped for his pistol. Catrinia cried out as the gun came to bear on her and his finger tightened on the trigger.

Chapter Nine

Catrinia let out a little squeal and scooted backward away from the gun. From the wild look in his eyes, she just knew Ferrell Cauruthers would shoot. He almost did. At the last instant, he threw the gun away, growling in disgust.

For a second, he stood there, his chest heaving. The whole episode shook him to the core. He had never even struck a woman, and just a few seconds ago, he'd come within a whisper of shooting one. He wiped his hand across his mouth, then pointed a shaky finger down at Catrinia Romanov. "Lady, have you gone plumb around the bend?" he yelled, wiping his hand across his mouth again. "I gotta notion to . . ." Ferrell paused, waving his arms and looking at the sky in exasperation. "Lady, you may wear big spurs where you came from, but around here, you ain't nothing. Ain't nobody coming to save you. If I were you, I'd just sit there and not move a muscle or make a sound."

Catrinia swallowed and nodded. Never in her life had anyone ever pointed a gun at her, and she found it an unnerving experience. Slowly she pulled the blanket up under her chin, watching with wide eyes as Cauruthers picked up his gun. He sat down and began to take the pistol apart. His long fingers moved gracefully as he carefully cleaned the weapon. From time to time, he would dab at the blood on his face and scowl darkly at her.

As the minutes wore on, the shock left her, and the silence began to grate on her nerves. "Mr. Cauruthers," she finally whispered.

"Lady, don't talk to me," Cauruthers answered, his voice tight. He made a vicious swipe at the blood on his face. "In case you missed it, I came within a whisker of shooting you. I feel low enough already. I don't need that on my conscience."

"Conscience?" Catrinia said sarcastically. "After the way you've treated me, I didn't suppose an animal like you had one. You jerked me off the stage, tied me like an animal and drug me halfway across the country, and yet you speak of having a conscience?"

"I'm sorry about that," Ferrell muttered, speaking straight at the ground. "Ain't much I can do about that now."

"You could release me!" Catrinia shot back.

Cauruthers snorted. "You wouldn't make it out of sight on your own," he told her.

"I might surprise you," she protested hotly, and Ferrell decided she might at that. She'd already shocked him a couple of times. She pulled at her hair, turning her head and looking at him out of the corner of her eyes. "I'm very sorry about your face. Does it hurt much?"

"No," Ferrell grunted, wary of whatever she might be up to.

"Did you mean what you said?" she asked coyly.

"How should I know? I can't even remember what I said," he grumbled.

"About feeling bad about all you've done to me?"

Ferrell suddenly found an interesting cloud in the sky and studied it a long time. "I ain't proud of what I done," he said finally.

"Then you could help me reach Whiskey City," she suggested, reaching out to touch his arm.

Ferrell swallowed hard, still looking at his cloud. He knew if he looked at her face, he'd cave in like a cheap mine shaft. "I told you, I can't. I gave my word."

Swearing, she kicked him on the shins. "I wish now that I would have clawed your eyes out!" she said and spat at him.

Ferrell yelped and rubbed his smarting shin, glaring at her with slitted eyes. "Lady, I swear, you're plumb loco."

Catrinia threw the blanket off, placing her hands on her hips. "There's no need to be insulting. And don't call me lady all the time."

"What do you want me to call you, your highness?" Ferrell asked snidely. "Well, lady, you can just forget about that. It's time you learned who's wearing the big bloomers here. I don't know what the devil got into you—" he started, but she cut him off.

"My dress was loosened," she said, stating each word coldly and clearly. "Maybe you would care to explain that?" His ears burning bright red, Ferrell Cauruthers suddenly took a powerful interest in cleaning his gun. Catrinia set her lips firm and crossed her arms over her chest. "I believe I asked you a question, Mr. Cauruthers."

Cauruthers groaned and swore quickly under his breath. "Shoot, lady, you fell off of that," he said, pointing to the twelve-foot-high embankment behind her. "I had to check and make sure you hadn't hurt yourself. Besides, you were all cinched up tighter than a bucking saddle. I figured you might suffocate. I just loosened them buttons a little."

For just an instant, Catrinia's face softened, but in a flash it was gone. "In the future, Mr. Cauruthers, I suggest you keep your hands to yourself. If I were you, I'd be worrying about my own welfare. I'll see that they hang you when they rescue me."

Ferrell Cauruthers threw down his gun and jumped to his feet. He stalked over to her, bending down into her face. "Lady, just who in the blazes do you think is coming to save you? Your so-called friends? They're the ones that paid me."

"Not Arkady. Arkady will come and you will be sorry," Catrinia said firmly. "Arkady loves me like a daughter."

"What the devil is an Arkady?" Cauruthers said with a grunt.

"Arkady Rostov, head of the Royal Palace Guards."

"Rostov," Cauruthers repeated with a sneer. He straightened up and waved a hand in her face. "You can just forget about him. Rostov was in on the deal from the start."

That rocked Catrinia's world to the core. She had been placing all of her hopes of rescue on Arkady Rostov's broad shoulders. She couldn't bear the thought that he might have betrayed her. "I don't believe you," she said defiantly, but her voice was a mere whisper.

Ferrell Cauruthers shrugged his shoulders and snatched the gun from the ground. "Suit yourself. Makes no never mind to me."

Catrinia couldn't bring herself to believe that Arkady would ever betray her. She clung to the hope that he was coming to save her like it was a lifeline. "You forgot to clean your gun," she pointed out, needling Cauruthers as a way to keep her mind occupied.

"Huh?" Cauruthers grunted as he kicked dirt onto the fire. "Lady, what the devil are you babbling about?" he asked, looking back at her.

"When you dropped your gun before, you stopped and cleaned it," she told him.

"Yeah, well, whatta you care?" he growled.

Catrinia laughed and shrugged. "I don't. I hope your gun is dirty and doesn't work. In fact, I hope when Arkady comes, he shoots you and you suffer greatly."

"Lady, I'm already suffering. There couldn't be anything worse than putting up with you," Cauruthers said, grumbling. "Now get on your feet. We're moving out."

"I thought you said we were waiting here," Catrinia reminded him.

"Lady, does this look like a good place to camp to you?"

"I know I've stayed in better places," Catrinia replied tartly. "But I must admit, it's better than where you picked last night. At least we are sheltered from the wind down here."

"Are you kidding?" Cauruthers hooted. "This is springtime in this here country. The last place you want to camp is down in a draw like this."

Catrinia felt a stab of pain from the jeering note in his tone. She set her jaw firm, determined not to ask anything of this crude ogre. Finally her curiosity won out over her pride. "Why isn't this a good spot?"

"Springtime, you get a lot of big, sudden rains. Flash floods are a common thing. You camp in a place like this and you're liable to wake up a hundred miles downstream."

"Where are we moving to?"

"There's a cabin on down the trail a couple of miles," Cauruthers answered, grunting a little as he swung his saddle up on his horse.

Catrinia sprang to her feet and stomped her foot into the dirt. "You mean to tell me that we slept out here on the cold, hard ground when there was a house nearby?"

"It ain't much of a house," Cauruthers said, snickering as he thought of what her reaction would be when she saw the place. "Besides, it got dark on us last night and I never been through this country before.'' This time he laughed outright. ''I reckon you found out what happens when you go to wandering around in the dark.''

Catrinia realized he was making fun of her, and when he chuckled again, her royal blood began to boil. Practically fuming, she watched through slitted eyes as he picked up the saddle for her horse. ''You might shake out those blankets and fold them,'' he instructed.

Catrinia folded her arms across her chest and glared at him. ''You want them blankets folded, I suggest you do it yourself.''

Ferrell Cauruthers looked at her, a smile tugging at his lips. ''Lady, you ain't running this show. Now, unless you want me to hog-tie you, shove a gag in your mouth, and sling you over that horse, get busy.''

''You wouldn't dare!'' Catrinia said, her eyes widening as she realized he might. She picked up the blankets and wadded them into a ball. ''There,'' she said, and flung the blankets in his face.

He let them hit him and fall to the ground. ''Do it right.''

Catrinia stuck out her tongue. ''Looks good to me. If it doesn't suit you, you can do it yourself!'' she said, sitting on a rock.

Ferrell looked at the wadded-up blankets at his feet and shook his head. ''I shoulda shot her,'' he mumbled to himself.

''Did you say something, Mr. Cauruthers?'' she called at him.

''Aw, be quiet. I swear, I never seen a more helpless

person in all my days,'' he griped, snatching the blankets from the ground and rolling them up so he could tie them behind his saddle.

By the time they were mounted and moving out of camp, Ferrell Cauruthers was exhausted. He felt like he'd been working a team of mules all day. One thing he had to admit about Catrinia Romanov, she could be pretty feisty when she took the notion.

As they rode, Ferrell began to think. He tried to calculate how long it would be until Fedarov came to take her off his hands. Ferrell didn't care for this whole deal. He figured the quicker Catrinia was gone, the quicker he could forget about it. Still, she was a pretty young lady. Despite himself, Ferrell stole a glance at her.

"Did you mean it when you said that being around me was torture? That you were suffering?" Catrinia asked suddenly. "Is my company so terrible?"

The question came out of nowhere and took Ferrell by surprise. He answered without thinking. "It ain't been a bed of roses."

A hurt look sprang into her eyes as she sniffled back tears. "I'm sorry to be such a burden on you."

"Aw, I'm sorry," Ferrell said with a groan. "I didn't mean it, but you could be a little more cooperative."

"I'm sorry, but I've never been kidnapped before. I don't know how one acts," she replied tartly. "You haven't exactly been pleasant company. You could let me go."

Ferrell Cauruthers hung his head, feeling lower than a

snake's basement. Every time she cried, he felt even lower. Somehow, Catrinia Romanov didn't fit his image of royalty. He'd always figured royal people were uppity, thinking they were better than everybody else. But she wasn't like that at all.

Ferrell knew he should do as she asked and take her into Whiskey City, but he'd given his word and taken Fedarov's money. Never in his life had Ferrell Cauruthers ever broken his word.

Ferrell glanced at her, chuckling at the tight set of her jaw. She had spunk, he'd give her that. She smelled nice too. Ferrell pulled the collar of his jacket up to his nose, inhaling the fresh scent of her hair that still clung to the coat.

When they finally reached the cabin, the sun had crossed halfway across the sky. "That's the place," Ferrell said, gesturing to the run-down cabin with his arm. "I hope you like it. He dismounted, circling around to her horse. He offered an arm up to her. "You go on inside. I'll tend the horses," he said.

He started to help her down, but she slapped his hand away. "I can manage on my own, thank you very much," she said.

"Suit yourself," Ferrell said with a shrug and a small chuckle.

Without a word, she marched stiffly up to the front door. Catrinia was being too cooperative, and that worried Ferrell. Taking no chances, he watched her until she disappeared inside. Keeping one eye on the cabin, Ferrell quickly stripped the saddles from the horses and turned the animals into the corral. He hung the saddles on the fence, taking his saddlebags as he walked up to the house. At the door, he stopped, scanning the country carefully. Seeing no danger, he went inside.

The first step into the cabin and he bumped into Catrinia, who stood frozen just inside the door. At the touch of their bodies, Ferrell Cauruthers felt a thrill shoot through him. Feeling warm all of a sudden, he took off his hat and edged past her. "Surveying your new court?" he asked, trying to make light of the situation.

A look of pure despair stamped on her delicate features, Catrinia tore her eyes from the mess stretched out in front of her. "You can't honestly expect me to set one foot into this hovel?" she asked, wrinkling up her nose. "This place is absolutely filthy."

Now, to be perfectly honest, Ferrell had to admit the place was a might on the dirty side. 'Course, he felt like he had the upper hand on her now, and he wasn't about to spoil it with being honest. "Don't look too bad to me," he said, prowling the room. "Why, there ain't even enough dirt on this tabletop to grow sorghum."

Catrinia placed her hands on her hips, her back ramrod straight and her eyes frosty. "That may be your criterion for determining cleanliness, but civilized people have much higher standards."

"No joking?" Pretending to be serious, Ferrell rubbed his chin. "You might have a point," he conceded. "I reckon if you think it needs a bit of dusting, you can hop to it. A little dirt never bothered me.'' Very pleased with himself, Ferrell crossed to the fireplace. He'd finally gotten Catrinia under control. Now he'd show her who was boss. He inspected the meager pile of wood against the wall, then loaded it in the fireplace. ''I'll stoke up a fire and you can stir us up something to eat. There's grub in my saddlebags.'' Ferrell smiled into the fireplace, sure that he finally had her under his thumb. He'd never been more wrong in his whole life.

Chapter Ten

As I saw that body, I jerked my horse to a stop and hissed a warning at Rostov. I needn't have bothered—that big Russian had already spotted it. For a surly galoot who always had his nose in the air, that ol' boy didn't miss much.

Without a word, we jerked our guns and fanned out, coming at the body from different sides. Despite our caution, no danger presented itself, and we met the body. We sat on our horses, looking down at the scene, learning what we could from the marks on the ground. From the tracks it was plain to see what had happened. The two riders had been moseying along just fine; then one of them shot the other in the back. It was a mighty casual thing that gave me a case of the chilblains. I mean he just up and shot, with no ryhme or reason that I could see. No warning either, and that's what bothered me.

A look of surprise showed on Arkady Rostov's face as he stared down at the dead man. "This man is no Russian," he said, a note of wonderment creeping into his gravelly voice.

Well, that much was obvious. I gave Rostov a hard look, still thinking if he knew something he wasn't telling me. "Did you expect it to be?" I asked, hoping to pry something out of him.

For a second, I thought the big son of a plowshare would clam up on me. His face thoughtful, he stared down at the body, then finally nodded. "Five men were supposed to accompany Catrinia at all times to ensure her safety. Since there was but one on that stage, I must conclude that something was wrong." He sighed heavily. "There is much unrest in my country. Every day many people go hungry. Some blame the czar and his family for this. I feared they might have taken their rage out on poor Catrinia."

"Well, this hombre was surely an American," I said, taking note of the high-heeled boots and wide hat. The man wore a gun belt, but whoever killed him had taken the pistol. I could see the tracks where the killer had knelt over the body.

"As I already said," Rostov said with a growl, like it was a big discovery. Muttering under my breath, I handed my reins to Rostov and swung down. "Surely, you do not intend to take time to bury this peasant?" Rostov demanded. "The princess's life could be in danger."

Now, I knew Rostov was right. Not that I liked admitting it one bit, but we couldn't spare the time to bury this man. Even though I knew all of this, it still didn't feel right to simply ride off and leave him lying in the grass. I mean, OK, he'd surely been in on the kidnapping, and was probably a varmint of the worst kind, but it still didn't set right. Frowning to myself, I bent down and went through his pockets.

"What do you do?" Rostov roared, sounding like a bear with a bad bicuspid. "Surely you do not rob the dead in this dreadful country?"

"'Course not!" I snapped, thinking I oughta splatter him one just for suggesting such a thing. I didn't whump him, but I sure enough gave that big Russian a high and mighty look while I explained it. "I was looking for something, a letter, maybe, anything that might tell me who he was. I reckon he has kin that would like to know what happened to him. Besides, if we knew who he was, we might find out who he runs with, and that might lead us to your princess."

For once, that danged big Russian hung his head and looked properly scolded. He waved a heavy arm at the body. "I apologize. Your actions are wise and correct. Please continue," he said gravely.

Now it was my turn to hang my head. Now that I'd finally put one over on the big son of a pump handle, it went and backfired on me. The dead man's pockets were drier than a drunk's throat on Sunday morning. "I already finished. His pockets done been cleaned out," I said in a small voice.

Now, I expected Rostov to sneer down his big nose at me, but he never done it. Instead, he got all grand on me. "No matter. Your thinking was sound," he said graciously. "Quite obviously, the killer thought of the same thing."

Now, I reckon, I just wasn't in the mood to be happy. I mean, if Rostov woulda gloated and said I told you so, which I fully expected him to do, I woulda been mad. The thing was, when he got all nice on me, that peeved me as well. "We lost some time. We best shake a leg," I said, standing up. I stomped over to my horse, then stopped, turning back for one last look at the dead man.

All of a sudden it occurred to me that these folks were downright serious. If we ever caught up to them, they'd put up a scrap. We might need all the firepower we could lay our paws on, and that dead man had a gun belt full of shells.

I didn't reckon he had a need for them so I hustled back over to the body and unbuckled the belt. As I pulled the belt from under his body, I saw that a name had been carved in the back of the leather. I held the belt up where I could read the name: Bill Paulson.

Ferrell Cauruthers was mad, frustrated, and bewildered all at the same time. He was on his hands and knees, scrubbing the floor like some kind of chambermaid.

He'd been cleaning for hours without a break. His back ached and sweat poured from his brow. He looked bleakly at his red, raw hands. Why, he'd built a fence for days and not scabbed up his hands like this.

Ferrell was confused. He hadn't wanted to clean.

Shoot, he'd never felt the desire to clean anything in his life. What confused him was how Catrinia had talked him into doing it. She had promised to cook, but that wasn't it. Besides, he'd been cleaning for hours and hadn't even gotten a whiff of food. From the looks of things he wasn't gonna either.

He glanced at Catrinia. She had appropriated the book from his saddlebags and now sat by the window, reading while he toiled.

Well, that did it!

Ferrell Cauruthers had had enough. His face flushing bright red, Ferrell threw his rag into the bucket of filthy water. By joe, a man could only take so much, and Ferrell had gotten a bellyful. After all, he was Ferrell Cauruthers, a hard, dangerous man. He was a man to be feared, and by gum he'd just mopped his last speck of dust.

"Lady, I want to talk to you," he said, growling.

Catrinia looked from her book and flashed him a dazzling smile. "Of course, Mr. Cauruthers," she said, laying the book aside. Moving with silky grace, she rose from the chair and glided across the room, inspecting his work. "I must say, you're doing a fine job," she said, congratulating him and favoring him with another smile.

A warmness spread through Ferrell's body and he completely forgot what he was going to say. "Why, thank you, ma'am," he mumbled, strangely pleased by her compliment.

Still smiling, she touched his shoulder, and the warm

feeling turned boiling hot. "Just a little more work and you'll have this place spotless."

"Yes, ma'am," Ferrell replied, unable to meet her gaze and looking at the floor. With a sudden movement, he snatched the rag from the bucket and went to scrubbing like a man possessed. He scrubbed for a full minute, before it dawned on him. She'd went and done it to him again!

A tremor of rage raced through his body. That low-down, double-dealing, conniving woman had tricked him again! The roar of rage that built up inside of him caught in his throat as the front door crashed open and a group of men rushed in. Black hoods were draped over their heads, hiding their faces.

The first man through the door grabbed Catrinia and slung her onto the bunk while the rest pointed their guns at Ferrell.

Ferrell rolled away from the bucket, his hand automatically sweeping for his pistol. When his hand reached his hip, Ferrell discovered his gun wasn't there. A feeling of dread settling heavily in his stomach, Ferrell looked at his gun belt on the table across the room.

Chapter Eleven

I held the pistol belt up for Rostov to see. He stared at it, then at me. "You know of this man Paulson?" he asked.

Now, I'd already been searching the back trails of my mind for a recollection of a man named Paulson, but I came up blank. I shook my head and crossed back to my horse. "We best get a move on it. That jasper and your princess got a good jump on us."

I hadn't meant to imply that Rostov had pulled a bonehead. Which, by the way, he had. He was the one that insisted we foller the wrong trail. Still, I hadn't meant to tromp on his feelings, but that's sure enough what I done. He didn't say a word for a long time, just stared straight ahead and fiddled with his reins.

"I was wrong not to listen to you," he said out of the blue. "Quite obviously, you were correct. You knew which trail we should follow and I'm sorry about not trusting your judgment."

Well now, if that was an apology, it sure snuck in the back door. I mean I noticed he never said anything about being sorry for calling me a rube, nor any of the other snooty things he said. "Ah, it's all right," I mumbled. I shifted in the saddle and scratched my chin. "Those men that were supposed to be guarding the princess. What you suppose happened to them?"

"I do not know." Rostov frowned and patted his horse's neck. "The leader of our party is a man named Boris Fedarov. He is an advisor to the czar."

"You sound like you don't trust this Fedarov hombre," I commented. I waited for a comeback, but Rostov snapped his jaws closed like a snapping turtle. I waited for a second, but Rostov didn't seem of a mind to answer my question, so I asked another. "How come you folks come out here anyway? Did you just get the urge to see Wyoming?"

"No, Fedarov came to Washington to finish the negotiations for the sale of Alaska from my country to yours."

"What's an Alaska?"

"A very large piece of land. Just north of your country. While your congress ratifies the proposed agreement, we came out here looking for a parcel of land to buy. The czar heard the hunting was good here. He wished to have an estate in this country."

"Why would your country want to sell this Alaska place to us? What is it? A desert?"

"No, from all I have heard, it is a place of extraordinary beauty." Rostov frowned, and I could tell he was choosing his words with care. "There is much poverty in my country. As I said, many people go hungry. My country needs money, and yours wants land, so a deal is struck.''

"So this czar hombre figures to pawn this chunk of ground off on us to raise himself some chips?"

"Yes. The czar wants to use this money to help ease the suffering of our people. Even so, there are many hard feelings toward the czar and his family."

"So you think some folks from your country snatched this princess?" I asked, then shook my head. "Naw, it don't hardly make sense. What would they be trying to accomplish?" I asked, thinking out loud, and thinking he had to be wrong. "Could they make this czar hombre back off and get themselves a new top dog?"

"Perhaps," Rostov said and grunted. "Maybe they think they can control the czar." Rostov's voice became hard and his face clouded with anger. "I fear they may harm Catrinia just to hurt the czar."

"They'd have to be some right nasty folks," I argued doubtfully. "We got some bad folks over here. If you ask me, a couple of outlaws took your princess and they'll want a pile of money to give her back."

Rostov didn't see it thataway, and believe me, that big Russian wasn't bashful about spouting his opinions. As a matter of fact, he spewed them out like a geyser. The thing was, we got jawing and let our guards drop.

We were backtracking to the spot where the kidnappers split up. Since we knew where we were going, we didn't pay as close attention as we shoulda. The upshot of it was, we blundered right into a vicious ambush.

The first shot drilled Rostov's horse right between the eyes. About an inch higher and that Russian would be taking harp lessons.

Without thinking, I dove headfirst out of the saddle and scrambled for cover. I didn't find much in the way of cover. Just a little depression where a small herd of buffalo bedded down one time and a few rocks. I sucked down to the ground, trying to keep my backside under cover, which wasn't easy. I didn't have much to hide behind, and my backside is mighty big.

As I caught my breath, I took stock of our situation. Rostov's horse was dead and the Russian was pinned underneath. Judging from the cussing I heard, I don't reckon Rostov was hurt, but he was sure trapped. He was right in the middle of the trail in plain sight. Whoever was shooting at us could finish him anytime.

Good sense told me there wasn't anything I could do for him. I'd vacated the saddle in a hurry and hadn't had time to nab onto my rifle. I had my pistol, but that dirty backshooter was way out of pistol range.

I looked over at Rostov, and knew I had to do something. Now, I didn't particularly care for the grumpy cuss, but I couldn't just stand by and watch him get killed.

As I floundered around and tried to brew up a dandy idea, that rifle crashed one more time. As the sound rolled through the hills like a locomotive, I saw the bullet thump into Rostov's body. His whole body jumped and a few drops of blood flew from his shoulder.

I'll give Rostov one thing, other than a small grunt, he never uttered a peep. His face was gray as he closed his eyes and clutched his wounded shoulder.

Right then, I knew we was in big trouble. That gent up ahead could shoot a mite. He was a good ways off, and in two shoots, he'd come within a whisker of sending Rostov over the great divide.

I had to come up with something mighty slick, but the only thing I could think of was charging, and that would get me killed in a hurry.

I groaned, knowing I was about to do something stupid. Now, it wasn't the first time, not by a long shot. 'Course, this time it was liable to get me killed.

Ferrell Cauruthers came off the floor in a rush, knocking his mop bucket flying in the process. Ignoring the guns trained at him, Ferrell jumped at the man who had thrown Catrinia into the bunk.

His big hand curled into a fist, Ferrell launched a roundhouse punch. Had that punch landed, it likely woulda took the man's head clean off, but Ferrell Cauruthers never got a chance to finish that punch. A rifle butt crashed into the side of his face, knocking him flying.

Ferrell staggered back, tripping over the bucket and sprawling on the dirty water that now covered the floor. The man who struck Ferrell leaped forward, reversing the rifle and smashing the muzzle painfully against Ferrell's throat. Hate gleaming in his eyes, the big man barked something that Ferrell couldn't understand.

Ferrell wiped at the blood trickling from his mouth. Ferrell coolly returned the stare of the bearlike man towering over him. "What did he say?" Ferrell asked of nobody in particular.

Before anyone could answer, a tall thin man strode calmly through the door. The man wore an expensive long coat and a contemptuous expression on his face. "Yuri said you should stick to scrubbing floors and leave the fighting to real men," Boris Fedarov said, peeling off a pair of soft, doeskin gloves.

"Fedarov!" Ferrell exclaimed. "I thought you were still in Laramie."

Fedarov gave a thin smile and removed his coat, handing the garment to the dark-skinned Yakov, who trailed him. "Well, as you can plainly see, you were mistaken. I am here."

A cold feeling inching up his spine, Ferrell looked past Fedarov and Yakov. "Where's Bill?" he asked, seeing no one behind them.

"Mr. Paulson won't be joining us," Fedarov said, crossing to the bunk, where Catrinia sat, cowering back in the corner. "I'm afraid Mr. Paulson is quite dead," Fedarov added, dismissing the thought with a wave of the gloves in his hand.

"You killed him?" Ferrell asked, his voice tight with grief and anger.

"Yakov did," Fedarov said and shrugged. "Mr. Paulson had outlived his usefulness."

"I'll kill both of you for that," Ferrell hissed.

Fedarov threw back his head and laughed out loud. "Mr. Cauruthers, if I were you, I would be worried about my own health," he said, looking at Catrinia. Holding the soft gloves in one hand, Fedarov clapped them lightly into the other hand as he stared at Catrinia. "Well, Duchess, I trust you are happy with your accommodations?" Fedarov bowed, sweeping the room with a wide gesture. "After all, this was arranged in your honor," Fedarov said with a biting laugh.

Her gray eyes wide with fear, Catrinia held her regal head high. "I do not know why you have chosen to do this, Boris Fedarov, but rest assured you shall stand in front of the firing squad. My father will see to that. By now, Arkady is already looking for me."

"Rostov," Fedarov sneered, caressing her face with the tips of the gloves. "By now, your precious Rostov is already dead," he taunted and slapped her face with the gloves. He smiled down at her, and it wasn't a pretty smile. "I dispatched Pavel to take care of him. You remember Pavel? Of course you do. Is he not the finest marksman in all of Russia, maybe the world?"

Catrinia choked back a sob, for she did indeed remember Pavel. Vividly she recalled the exhibition the man put on for her father last summer. Pavel had shot at targets all afternoon and hadn't missed once. A single tear welled up in her eye and rolled down her cheek. In a flash, a wave of memories flooded her mind. How Arkady used to carry her through the snow when she was young and how safe she felt in his strong arms.

Ferrell Cauruthers didn't care about Arkady Rostov, but it tore his heart in two to see the pain etched so deeply on Catrinia's delicate features. His hands trembling from frustration, Ferrell tensed himself, a growl of rage rolling past his lips. Immediately, the man guarding Ferrell pressed the rifle even harder against Ferrell's throat, leaning his bulk into the task.

The dark-faced Yakov stepped up next to Fedarov. "Let's kill him now. We no longer need him," Yakov suggested, his eyes gleaming.

Smiling tightly, Fedarov knelt beside Ferrell. "Yakov is right. You have served your purpose and outlived your usefulness. Perhaps you can think of a reason that I shouldn't kill you?"

Ferrell had already come to the conclusion that if they wanted to kill him, then they would and he wasn't going to give them the satisfaction of begging. Instead of answering, he merely glared at Fedarov.

The man holding the rifle to Ferrell's throat said something in Russian and then let out a booming laugh. Fedarov laughed as well, cocking his head off to one side as he studied Ferrell. "Yuri says you are a coward and not to be feared. He says you are fit only for women's work and that we should allow you to finish your scrubbing, then kill you. What do you think of that, Mr. Cauruthers?"

Ferrell spat in Yuri's direction. "You stack that rifle in the corner and I'll mop the floor with you!"

Yuri Cheneko was ready to take Ferrell up on the offer, when Fedarov interrupted with a savage sweep of his hand. "*Nyet!*" he said harshly. "No, Mr. Cauruthers, you are going to do me a favor. You do it well and perhaps I will spare your life."

"I wouldn't spit on you if you was on fire," Ferrell sneered.

An amused look on his face, Fedarov laced his fingers together, looking over them at Ferrell. "Oh, I think you will," he predicted smugly.

"Don't bet on it, scarecrow," Ferrell said calmly, but inside he was wary. The Russian was too sure of himself. Ferrell was afraid he had something up his sleeve.

For an answer, Fedarov turned and crossed to Catrinia's bunk. He cupped her chin in his hand. She twisted away from him and would have slapped him, but he easily caught her flying hand. "Unless you want something terrible to happen to our dear Czaritsa, you'll do exactly as you are told!"

Ferrell was a poker player and he knew the value of a good bluff. Trying to appear casual, he snorted and waved a hand at Catrinia. "Go ahead. Kill her for all I care. She ain't been nothing but a pain in the rear end."

The anger that snapped and crackled from Catrinia's gray eyes as she glared at Ferrell in shock could have leveled mountains. The torrent of angry words that started to flood past her lips stopped as Fedarov threw back his head and laughed.

"Bravo, Mr. Cauruthers," he said, clapping his hands. "A very fine performance. You almost convinced me."

All the laughter drained off his face so fast that it was hard to imagine it was ever there in the first place. He pointed a long finger at Ferrell. "You will deliver a message to the authorities, telling them we demand one hundred thousand dollars for the safe return of Grand Duchess Catrinia."

Fedarov wheeled quickly, snatching Catrinia by the wrist and dragging her bodily from the bunk, slapping her hand down on the table. "To prove to the authorities we have the duchess, you will take her ring with her family crest on it." Fedarov barked a quick order to Yakov, who grinned and pulled a long, curved knife from his sash.

As Fedarov spoke, Catrinia let out a squeal of fear and tried to twist away from him. She might have made it, but two of the Russian guards jumped forward, grabbing her and helping Fedarov force her hand back on the tabletop. Fedarov swiveled his head to look at Ferrell. "And to show them that we mean business, you will take the finger where the ring rests."

As Fedarov finished speaking, Yakov raised the knife, wiping a speck off the blade.

Chapter Twelve

Elmo done decided that kids oughta be penned up like hogs. The way he saw it, you could lock them up when they were born and turn them out when they were full grown and had good sense.

Elmo scratched at the whiskers on his lean cheeks and glanced sourly at Stevie Hunt. Dang little horse apple! Stevie knew where the kidnappers were holding that princess and he wasn't telling. Elmo had tried threats and the little worm just laughed at him. Right then, Elmo decided to change tactics. If he couldn't scare the location out of the little puddle jumper, then he'd trick it out of him.

Elmo allowed himself a little smile. This was gonna be easy pickin's. He adjusted the hat on his head, then turned and smiled at the little mud ball. "Say, Stevie, little buddy," Elmo cooed, his voice dripping with honey. "How much farther do you reckon it is to where they got that princess stashed?" he asked innocently.

"A ways," Stevie replied, shooting a knowing look at Elmo. "Why do you ask?"

Elmo shrugged, reaching out and patting the youngster on the back. "Well, you know, I got to thinking"— Elmo had to stop and choke back a chuckle over his own cleverness—"if it ain't far, we could push on. 'Course, if we got a ways to go yet, we might as well stop and rest the horses a bit. Might even fix us a bite of grub."

Like a snake striking, Lester's head snapped up and around. "Eat? Did you say eat?" he asked, smacking his lips eagerly.

Elmo scowled bleakly and whacked his brother. "There ain't no need in stopping if we're already there." Elmo looked slyly at the youngster. "How's about it, son? Are we almost there?"

"I don't care how far it is. I want to eat now!" little Jenny put in.

"Be quiet, little missy," Elmo snapped, shaking his finger in Jenny's face, which was the wrong thing to do.

Jenny promptly bit his finger. "Don't you tell me to shush," she said after releasing his finger.

Elmo never heard her, he was too busy shaking his injured finger and roaring at the top of his lungs. "Why, you little pip-squeak, I oughta . . . ."

Elmo was fighting to nab a grip on his temper, when Stevie's quiet voice reached him. "It's a ways," the youngster said and pulled his horse to a stop. "I reckon we might as well stop and eat."

Elmo swore bitterly. He didn't want to stop and eat. He wanted to push on. They didn't have time for this nonsense, there was money to be made. "Aw, just forget it. Let's keep moving," he grumped.

"Come on, Elmo, let's stop. I'm real hungry," Lester pleaded, clasping his hands in front of his face. "Please."

"No," Elmo snapped. "I'm running this here show and I say we keep going."

Elmo kicked his horse into motion, but the others refused to move. After several yards he glanced back over his shoulder. "Well, ain't you comin'?"

"We're stopping to eat. You can go on if you like. We'll catch up to you," Stevie said.

"Yeah, we're stopping," Jenny seconded, pointing a finger at Elmo. "You just go on."

Elmo swore bitterly. He was sorely tempted to throttle both of the little varmints. He tried to keep in mind that he needed Stevie, but it wasn't easy. With a groan, he gave in. "All right, we'll stop and eat," he agreed, but it came out through clenched teeth.

As they dug through their saddlebags, Elmo sidled up to Stevie. "Boy, we's partners. Ain't right that you should hold out on your partners."

His face serious, Stevie nodded. "I been thinking on that, and I reckon you're right. The place they're holding that princess is about half a day's ride straight west."

"They just holed up out in the middle of nowhere?" Elmo asked suspiciously.

"They said there was a cabin," Stevie replied.

"A cabin? No foolin'?" Elmo muttered, rubbing his chin thoughtfully. Deciding that Stevie was giving him the straight goods, Elmo broke into a smile. "You're a good lad,'' he said, ruffling Stevie's hair. ''Now, let's eat.''

As the others feasted on jerky and stale biscuits, Elmo hissed at Lester and jerked his head off to the side. ''What's the matter, Elmo? Did you spring a leak?'' Lester asked, mumbling around a mouthful of biscuit.

''Get over here!'' Elmo snapped, dragging Lester away from the kids. Once they were a safe distance away, Elmo looked over Lester's shoulder, watching them kids. ''You know, I been thinking,'' he said. ''What do we need them brats for?''

''We don't know where they got the old gal stashed. How are we gonna find her if we don't have Stevie to show the way?'' Lester said, worried.

''I wormed a few details outta the kid. Don't you fret, I can sniff out the princess,'' Elmo said, popping his suspenders.

''We might need that kid. He's right savvy,'' Lester whined.

Elmo smiled and clapped his brother on the back. ''We don't need him. We're pretty foxy ourselves.''

A toothy grin broke across Lester's face. ''I reckon you're right about that,'' he said. ''We pulled some mighty slick jobs in our time.''

''You dang betcha we did,'' Elmo agreed. ''And we didn't need no runny-nosed kid to help us neither.''

Stevie chewed on his jerky and watched the two brothers. He didn't have to hear them to know what they were saying. They were plotting to ace him and Jenny out of the deal. Stevie smiled and took another bite. He had some ideas of his own.

He wasn't at all surprised when Elmo announced that he and Lester were leaving them behind. Stevie didn't put up an argument, he just chewed his jerky and watched them go.

"Are we going back to town now?" Jenny asked as the two brothers disappeared from sight.

"No," Stevie decided. "We'll go after that princess our ownselves."

"How are we gonna beat them there?" Jenny asked, ready to do anything her brother did.

Stevie smiled. "They are going the wrong way. I sent them straight west. The cabin where the princess is at is south and west of here. They'll never find it. Finish eating, and let's go."

As the morning turned into afternoon and evening came, Elmo realized he'd been duped. That two-timing brat had sent them on a wild-goose chase. For an hour Elmo had been swearing and grinding his teeth. Now he was beyond words.

As they pulled into the shade of a small stand of cottonwoods, Lester took off his hat, shaking his head. "That's the trouble with youngsters these days, they ain't honest," he said solemnly, and completely forgetting that he and Elmo hadn't been honest a day in their lives. "They got no respect for their elders neither."

"Be quiet, Lester. I'm trying to think," Elmo growled, swinging down. Folding his arms across his chest, he stomped around in small circles, muttering to himself.

*   *   *

I'd just about given me and Rostov up for dead. He was pinned under his horse and there wasn't any way I could help him. Nor could I leave him. And believe me, I dang sure considered it. I figured that maybe I could crawl on my belly and sneak away. I couldn't bring myself to do it, though. Even after all the nasty things he'd said to me, I couldn't tuck my tail and slink off, leaving him to die.

The way I saw it, we had one chance, but that chance was slimmer than a salt-flat cow. What I figured to do was slip around behind this gent and give him a taste of his own medicine.

I figured he'd be ready for this maneuver, but I was gonna give 'er a go. I rubbed the pistol resting in my big paw. I'd have to get mighty close to have a hope of scoring a hit. If I missed, or he spotted me along the way, I was a dead man and so was Rostov.

To tell the truth, I didn't have much hope of pulling it off, but I done decided that I'd just as soon go down scraping and clawing. Yes, sir, I'd given us up for dead, but I'd forgotten about Rostov.

Just as I was screwing up my nerve, Rostov hissed at me. "What do you want?" I whispered back, a little put out at him for snapping my concentration.

For an answer, Rostov made a little pointing gesture with his good hand. When I saw what he was pointing at, my eyes nearly bugged right outta my head. Now for an ol' boy whose noggin looked like an adobe brick,

Rostov sure enough had some mush between his ears. What's more, he'd been using it too.

Somehow, he'd snaked his rifle out of the saddleboot. That Winchester lay beside him, shielded from the bushwhacker by Rostov's chunky body. As I watched him, he hooked the fingers of his good hand around that shooter and gave it a flip.

Well, right up to then, I'd been right proud of that hardheaded Russian, but he sure flubbed it. When he flipped that rifle, he didn't put enough oompf behind the toss and it landed a good three feet short.

Only three feet, but the dang thing might as well have been on the moon. To get it, I was gonna have to stick my head out. And while I'll grant you that I'm not the most handsome feller who ever came along, I liked my head just the way it was. Anyway, I didn't figure a hole between my eyes would make me any prettier.

I growled a few cusswords at that Russian for not getting the rifle to me, then I got down to business. I got to thinking that if I had something, maybe a stick, I could snake that rifle over to me. I glanced around me for a stick or something, but there wasn't one to be found.

A feeling of desperation creeping up my spine, I beat my fists into the ground, my eyes darting back and forth. It didn't make any difference. No matter how much I looked and squirmed, I couldn't find a thing.

Now, they say that desperation is like a pair of big-rowled spurs digging into your brain. I reckon they're right, 'cause my brain lumbered to life and I brewed myself an idea. It wasn't anything earthshaking. What I figured to do was slip off a boot and use it to drag that shooter over to me.

'Course, that proved to be easier said than done. I don't know if you've ever tried to peel off a boot while hunkered down behind a small rock, but it ain't easy. Somehow, I accomplished the feat and got that boot off. Ignoring the green fog rolling out of the boot, I reached out for that rifle. I'd just hooked the toe in the trigger guard, when a shot rang out. That sorry son of a blunderbuss shot a hole plumb through my boot.

When that bullet smacked into my boot, I jerked back like I'd been scalded. Somehow, in that jerk, I hauled that rifle over to me. Tossing that boot away, I snagged onto that rifle with both hands. Now me and my attacker were on even terms.

Just as I realized that, I realized something else. Now that I had that rifle, Rostov was in real danger. The killer wouldn't want to take a chance on Rostov getting out from under his horse. He wouldn't want to take on both of us at the same time. He'd try and finish Rostov off now.

I shot to my feet, just in time to see the bushwhacker sighting over the top of his rock, taking dead aim at Rostov. Without thinking or even aiming, I fired from the hip. To tell the truth, I'd have been tickled pink if I'd smoked that polecat right between the eyes. Well, that never happened, but my bullet did whack against that rock in front of him and sent the varmint to huntin' a hole.

While that sorry bugger had his tail tucked, I figured to make my move. Paying no attention to the fact that I only had one boot, I charged. Holding the rifle at my hip, I roared up the slope, firing as I ran.

Not that he was close enough to do any good, but Rostov opened up with his pistol. We were doing a right fair job of keeping that bushwhacker's head, when it all came apart on us and tragedy smacked us right in the whiskers.

Chapter Thirteen

When they cut back over their own tracks, Stevie
pulled his horse to a stop. Feeling his eyes burn, Stevie
fought the panic that threatened to rush over him.

"Stevie, I'm hungry," Jenny said, tugging at his
sleeve. "It's getting cold too."

"I know. We'll find that cabin any minute," Stevie
said with a lot more hope than conviction.

"I don't want to do this anymore. I want to go back
into town," Jenny said, beginning to pout.

Stevie wanted to go into town as well; the problem
was, Stevie wasn't quite sure which way town was.
They'd been going in circles, and now Stevie was a little
bewildered. Back home, he'd known the country inside
and out. Getting lost was never a problem there, and
today the thought of losing his way never occurred to
Stevie. But this country all looked the same to him. It
was so confusing.

Swallowing the acid-tasting lump in his throat, Stevie
fought back the tears and tried to think. He couldn't help
but wish they'd stayed back in Whiskey City, but Stevie

had wanted to show off. Stevie liked showing off. He liked doing things nobody thought a pack of kids could pull off. The fact that these things were bad didn't bother Stevie; in fact, that just added spice to the adventure.

"Stevie, are we lost?" Jenny wailed, tears tracking down her dirty little cheeks.

Stevie closed his eyes and nodded. He'd just wanted to have a little fun and get a little attention. He hadn't bargained for all of this. It was going to be dark in a few hours, and then they would be in real trouble.

His whole life, Ferrell Cauruthers had been scrapping and clawing just to get by. Over the years, he'd gotten himself into some real tight spots, and in the process, he'd stumbled on a few dirty tricks. He wasn't squeamish about using them.

As Yakov held his knife up, a rage built in Ferrell. He glanced at big Yuri, who had let his guard down. Instead of watching Ferrell, Yuri's attention was on the grisly drama at the table.

That little opening was all Ferrell needed. Still seated on the floor, he rocked back, drawing his feet into him. Using all his power, Ferrell lashed out. His booted feet smashed Yuri on the side of the knee. Howling like a branded hound, Yuri toppled to the floor. As the giant Russian fell toward him, Ferrell lashed out with a short wicked punch. Yuri fell right into the punch, his weight more than doubling the impact. His jaw broken, Yuri crashed to the floor and lay silent.

Even before Yuri completed his fall, Ferrell snatched the pistol from his sash. Spinning on the floor, Ferrell came to one knee ready to fire, but could not for fear of hitting Catrinia. The Russians, startled by his sudden attack, were just now springing into action. The two bodyguards had released their hold on Catrinia and were stepping sideways to get a shot at Ferrell. Fedarov jerked Catrinia close to him, using the princess as a shield in case Ferrell opened up.

Ferrell couldn't fire for fear of hitting her. Instead, he lunged across the tiny room. Ferrell dove at Yakov, who had also tried to use Catrinia as a shield, only to have his boss jerk her away from him. Yakov sensed the attack coming and tried to spin and bring his knife to bear. He was a second too slow.

Ferrell barreled into the smaller man, his shoulder catching the Russian in the short ribs. Ferrell's weight slammed Yakov back into the wall with enough force to shake dirt from the rafters. Yakov let out a long wheezing grunt as the knife clattered from his fist. A sudden fury seizing him, Ferrell upped his knee into Yakov's midsection, lifting the smaller man off the ground.

Yakov's two friends had their guns out, but now it was their turn to hold their fire, as Yakov was in their line of fire. Ferrell grabbed Yakov in a bear hug and charged. Using Yakov's body like a battering ram, Ferrell plowed into the pair. One of the bodyguards went down, pinned under Yakov's body. The other staggered back, tangling his feet in an overturned chair and crashing heavily to the ground.

As Ferrell whirled to help the princess, he saw she was doing all right on her own. She'd managed to twist away from Fedarov, the long, deep scratches on his face testimony as to how she pulled that off. She didn't show any signs of wanting to get away. Right then, she looked of a mind to do some more damage.

Before she had a chance to try, Ferrell shoved Fedarov back and grabbed her by the arm. Almost dragging her along, Ferrell sprinted for the door. The bodyguard who'd tripped over the chair had gotten to his feet and made a feeble attempt to stop them. Without slowing down, Ferrell lashed out with the pistol in his fist. The tip of the front sight ripped across the man's forehead, leaving a bloody gash.

As they burst out the front door, Ferrell looked for the Russians' horses. The animals were standing in the yard, tied to a small tree. Ramming the pistol down in his jeans, Ferrell boosted Catrinia into the saddle, practically throwing her onto the nearest horse. Flipping the reins to her, Ferrell slapped the horse on the rump.

As Catrinia's horse pounded away, one of the bodyguards burst out the door of the cabin, a pistol in his hand and his eyes searching for Ferrell.

They saw each other at the same time, but Ferrell was the quicker of the two. Before the Russian could swing his gun to bear, Ferrell snapped his pistol out of his belt and fired. Ferrell fired as the gun came level, pulling the trigger three times. The slugs from that gun drove the Russian back to the door, where he collapsed.

Ferrell didn't want to stick around and see what was gonna happen next. With quick jerks, he untied all of the horses, holding onto one and shooing the others away. Swinging into the saddle, Ferrell snapped a quick shot at the door of the cabin, then pounded after Catrinia.

A few shots followed Ferrell, but he didn't stop to fight back. Instead, he fired the last shot in his pistol over the heads of the fleeing horses, hoping to scatter them.

Ferrell ran his horse for a mile and he still hadn't caught Catrinia. Looking ahead, he could see a small cloud of dust raised by her running horse. Ferrell stared at the cloud, willing her to slow down. She had to slow down before she ran the animal out.

Ferrell knew Fedarov and his men would be coming after them, and with no bullets, Ferrell wasn't going to put up much of a fight. They had to make a run for it. It was a long ways to help, and Ferrell wasn't placing any bets on them giving the Russians the slip. It might come down to outrunning them. Something they wouldn't be able to do if Catrinia's horse was played out. Ferrell cursed himself for turning the rest of the horses loose; he should have brought them along. Fresh mounts to switch to might make all the difference.

He couldn't change what had already been done, so Ferrell tried to make the best of it. He pulled his horse down into a ground-eating canter, hoping Catrinia would do the same. An impatience chewing at him, Ferrell kept an eye on the tiny plume of dust ahead of him. He also kept a sharp watch behind him. So far, no pursuit showed, but Ferrell took no comfort in that. He'd barked them up some, but them Russians were tough men. They were playing for high stakes and Ferrell knew they would shake off their hurts and come fuming up the trail with blood in their eyes.

Another mile fell behind them and Ferrell saw that Catrinia was finally slowing down. A few minutes later she stopped in a small grove of cottonwoods, and he caught her. The relief he felt was short-lived as he saw the reason she stopped. A pair of guns aimed right at her.

Chapter Fourteen

Ferrell Cauruthers pounded into the stand of trees, then jerked his horse to a stop when he saw the two rough-looking men holding their guns on Catrinia. Very much aware that his pistol was empty, Ferrell decided to reason with these men. "I'm glad to see you fellers. We need help," he told them. "This is Princess Catrinia Romanov from Russia. She was kidnapped and we just escaped."

A look of slow wonderment spread across the long face of one of the men, as he let out a low whistle. "Well, whadda you know, Elmo? That little whippersnapper was right."

"Shut up, Lester," Elmo commanded. Pushing Lester aside, Elmo begin to pace, scratching his backside as he looked from Catrinia to Ferrell. "We know who she is. What we don't know is who you are. Why don't you swing down and tell us?"

Ferrell looped his reins around the saddle horn and returned Elmo's gaze. When Ferrell didn't answer immediately, Lester jumped forward and went to jabbing the bigger man with his rifle. "You heard the man, green-horn. Pile down off that horse 'fore I have to get rough with you!" Lester threatened. As Ferrell swung down, Lester scurried back several steps, but as soon as Ferrell was down, Lester was back, poking and prodding with his rifle. "Okay, hoss, speak up. What's your name?"

"Ferrell Cauruthers. I'm helping the—"

"Never heard of you," Elmo said with a flip of his hand. "Lester, take his gun."

"The gun is empty," Ferrell said through tight lips.

Lester snorted and gouged Ferrell in the ribs. "What do you take us for, a couple of yahoos?" Lester growled surly. "We ain't falling for that old empty gun trick. Now fork over that beanie shooter 'fore I blast you."

Ferrell sighed, wondering what fell on these two. It had to be something heavy enough to deaden their brains. As he glanced over at Catrinia, he saw a smile flirting on her lips. Well, good thing she thought all of this was funny, because Fedarov and his men would be on them any minute.

Ferrell turned back to the men in front of him. "Look, we really don't have time for all of this," Ferrell said, spreading his hands in front of him. "We have some mighty bad men after us. If you won't help us, at least let us pass. Believe me, these are tough men following us, and you don't want to tangle with them."

Elmo squared his scrawny shoulders and hiked up his gun belt. "We're a couple of salty dogs our ownselves. These hombres give us any trouble and we'll send them packing with their backsides scalded,'' Elmo allowed, as Ferrell groaned and cut his eyes up to the sky. Hiking up his gun belt again, Elmo glared fiercely at Ferrell. ''Now, are you gonna pass over that shooter, or do we have to get rough with you?''

''I could smoke the polecat if you want,'' Lester offered, gouging his rifle under Ferrell's arm.

''Go ahead and try,'' Ferrell growled, slapping the rifle away.

Lester jerked the rifle in close to his body and backpedaled over by his brother. ''Did you see that?'' Lester sputtered, waving the rifle. ''That sorry slop bucket is giving me back talk.''

''I'll handle this,'' Elmo volunteered. Hooking his thumbs in his shell belt, he strutted over to Ferrell. ''You're just about to get me riled up. Now pass over that shooter 'fore we have to rough you up some.''

Catrinia let out a little laugh, then quickly covered her mouth with her hand. ''Just give him the gun,'' she urged between giggles.

Ferrell didn't like it, but he passed the pistol over to Lester. Even though the weapon had been empty, Ferrell had felt better just having it. Ferrell didn't know who these men were or what they wanted, but he had little faith in their ability to go against Fedarov and his goons.

Lester poked the pistol in his belt, then grinned at Ferrell. ''Now you're showing some smarts,'' he said, then waved with his rifle. ''Get over there with the pretty lady and don't try anything. I got an itchy trigger finger.'' He followed Ferrell's movements with his rifle, then when they were together, Lester turned to his brother. ''Now what do we do?''

Elmo frowned and spat on the ground. ''Don't rightly know,'' he admitted, scratching his belly as he paced. Now that they had the princess, Elmo didn't know what to do next. Despite himself, Elmo almost wished Stevie Hunt was here. The little leach was a pain, but the kid seemed to have things figured out. Elmo scrunched up his eyebrows and picked at the seat of his britches as he tried to think. They had the princess, but now what? They wanted a ransom, but whom did they ask to give it? Likely that kid would know. All of a sudden, Elmo realized, the princess would know.

A smile breaking across his horse face, Elmo marched right up to the pair. A dignified expression on his face, he looked gravely at the pair. ''All right, we don't want to kill you, but as you can see we're a pair of mighty rough hombres. We'd kill you like that,'' he said and tried to snap his fingers, but they didn't pop. Swearing quickly under his breath, Elmo put his fingers together and worked them into snapping position. ''Like that!'' he yelled and tried to snap them again, with the same results as before.

''Here, let me do 'er for you,'' Lester offered, stepping forward and snapping his fingers under Elmo's nose.

''Would you get away from me!'' Elmo howled, slapping furiously at Lester's hand.

A delightful laugh escaping past her lips, Catrinia

turned away, resting her head on Ferrell's shoulder. Ferrell fought to keep a straight face, very much aware of her touch. He could smell her hair and all of a sudden, he had the urge to put his arm around her. It seemed like a natural thing to do, but Ferrell resisted. After all, Catrinia Romanov was a princess and Ferrell just a cowhand.

His face the color of cactusberry jam, Elmo shoved Lester away from him and jerked out his gun. He held the weapon up for everyone to see. "You think this is funny, sister?" he squawked, making jabbing motions with the pistol. "I bet you wouldn't be laughing if I plugged your boyfriend."

Holding her fingers to her lips and managing to look solemn, Catrinia raised her head from Ferrell's shoulder and turned back to face Elmo. "I am sorry, Mr. Elmo. Please continue with what you were saying."

"Huh?" Elmo grunted, his face looking foggy. He pursed his lips and scratched under his arm with the muzzle of the pistol. "Oh, yeah. Like I was saying, you do what you're told and you won't get hurt. You cross us and we'll snuff the both of you." Elmo paused and whipped the gun up into firing position. "You savvy that?" he demanded.

Both Catrinia and Ferrell tried their best to look somber as they nodded. Ferrell pretty much pulled it off, but Catrinia cracked and let out a small snicker.

His face flaming, Elmo jumped up and down, flapping his arms wildly. "You stop laughing!" he screamed. "I swear, I'll snuff you!"

"Don't do that!" Ferrell cried, cringing as Elmo waved the pistol. Dang fool was gonna kill them by mistake. "She ain't trying to make fun of you. I reckon you got her scared plumb silly."

Ferrell's words pleased Elmo. Sniffing loudly, he crammed the pistol back down in the holster. He looked seriously into Catrinia's eyes, then nodded. "I reckon you're right," he agreed, his chest puffing out. He looked to Ferrell, then cut his eyes to the sky. "Women," he said knowingly.

"I think if you keep that gun in the holster, she'll be all right," Ferrell said, then glanced sternly at Catrinia. "Ain't that right?"

This time, Catrinia managed to more or less keep a straight face. "Dear me, yes," she said, fanning a hand in front of her face. "Those guns, they frighten me so."

"You just do what we say and we won't have to use them," Elmo said, feeling grand. "Now, we ketched you fair and square and we figure to sell you back to your people." Elmo paused, scratching his chin and staring up at the sky. "We want five, no, make it ten thousand, to give you back."

"Ten thousand dollars!" Lester exclaimed. He swallowed hard, then had to sit down on a stump. "Lordy, I ain't never seen that much money in all my days!" He gulped down another deep breath, then glared suspiciously at Catrinia. "Your kin got that much jack?"

"Yes," Catrinia answered excitedly. "If you gentlemen will escort us into Whiskey City, I'll see that you get your money."

"Lady, do we look like a couple of saps to you?" Elmo asked, his tone biting. "If we was to take you into Whiskey City, the first thing you would do is sic that big sheriff on us."

"We don't like that sheriff, " Lester explained. He frowned at the ground, concentrating hard. "Elmo, how are we gonna get the money?"

"I working on it," Elmo replied. He glanced at Catrinia out of the corner of his eye. "Who would we have to see about the money?"

"A man named Arkady Rostov."

"Good," Elmo grunted, then turned back to his brother.

"Lester, you haul into Whiskey City and find this Rostov. Shake the money out of him, then hustle right back."

"I think the princess's idea was the best," Ferrell put in quietly. "Are you forgetting about the men following us? They're gonna be coming soon."

"You know, I don't see any men behind you. Besides, we got it on good authority that four of you hit the stage, and that you split up and two of you went south," Elmo said, remembering what Stevie told him. "I think you just made up them men chasing you to try and spook us," Elmo declared, then looked at his brother. "But me and Lester don't spook easy. Do we, Lester?"

"No, siree, Bob," Lester agreed, slapping at his holstered gun. "Ain't much in this whole wide world scares us."

"That's right," Elmo seconded. "All right, Lester, get your horse and head for Whiskey City."

Lester frowned and jerked his hat down. He traced a circle in the dirt with the toe of his boot. "I don't want to go," he mumbled, hanging his head.

"What do you mean you don't want to go?" Elmo demanded fiercely.

"That mean old hag with the buffler gun lives in Whiskey City. She don't like us and she scares me."

Iris Stevens scared Elmo a little too, but he wasn't about to admit it. "Bah," he grunted, waving his hand. "That old bat is all talk. She ain't about to shoot anyone."

"Last time we saw her, she seemed awful set on the notion. I reckon she'd do it too, if we gave her half a chance," Lester complained.

"Lester, I swear, you're turning into a regular fraidy cat," Elmo jeered. "Now, when in your life did you ever hear of some old gray-haired granny shooting anybody?"

Lester scratched his head and stared at the ground. "Well, I never heard tell of it, but that don't mean it couldn't happen, and I don't want to be the first," Lester declared, crossing his arms and poking his lower lip out. "If you ain't scared, you can just go yourself."

Elmo didn't like it one bit, but he couldn't back down. Instead, he tried to talk his way out. "You sure you can handle these two? That princess looks tough, she might come at you with a hairpin."

"Aw, I can handle them, you just go on," Lester replied.

Elmo hesitated, then stalked stiffly to his horse. "I'm going, but I want you to keep an eye on these two. If they get away, I'll peel your sorry hide."

"You betcha, I'll watch 'em with both eyeballs," Lester promised as Elmo swung aboard his horse. "Say, Elmo, how's about bring me back a hunk of hourshound?"

Elmo swore quickly. "I ain't stopping to get you no candy," he said flat out. "And I'm warning you, these two best be here when I get back!" His threat hanging in the air, Elmo wheeled his horse around and galloped away.

Lester watched his brother until Elmo was out of sight, then spun around to face his two prisoners. "Well, looks like I'm the big cheese now," he said. Holding his gun belt up with both hands, Lester marched back and forth in front of his captives. "All right, dig the wax outta your ears, 'cause I'm only gonna say this once." Lester gave his gun belt another hitch, squared back his shoulders and puffed out his thin chest. "You try anything cute and *blap!* You're dead!" he shouted, whirling and whipping out his pistol. "You savvy that?" he asked, and Catrinia and Ferrell both nodded solemnly. "Yeah, I though you would," Lester crowed.

Ferrell watched closely as Lester flipped the gun back down into the holster and resumed his pacing. Ferrell had to shake his head. He'd never came across a denser pair in all his life. Ferrell shunted his eyes sideways, looking in the direction Elmo took. Elmo was out of sight, but Ferrell decided to wait just a few more minutes. Ferrell had already decided to take Lester. Ferrell hoped he didn't have to hurt the little man, because in a way, Ferrell kinda liked him.

Lester was still pacing, laying out his ground rules. "Now, I don't wanna have to put up with a lot of gum flapping. You want to exercise your jaws, chew on a dirt clod, but do it quiet like."

Lester stopped strutting, patting his belly with both hands. "Yes, sir, I'm a-runnin' this here show," he said, running a finger along his jaw. "You got any notions and you best tell them to vamoose. I ain't smoked nobody this week, but I'm itching to," he warned and began his strutting again. "You try anything, and *bang!*"

This time, when Lester whirled and pulled his gun, he got a bit more than he bargained for. Somehow, he managed to pull the trigger. The gun went off suddenly, startling everyone. As Lester dropped the pistol and jumped back, Ferrell Cauruthers slowly melted to the ground.

Chapter Fifteen

With a roar, I charged that bushwhacker like I thought I was ten men. Right then, I figured to ramble right up to him, ram my rifle down his throat, and jerk the trigger. To tell the truth, I kinda forgot I only had one boot. Then I stomped down on a sharp rock and was reminded.

When I came down on that sharp rock, my whole leg felt like it'd been seared by a branding iron. My knee buckled and I plowed snootfirst into the ground. Somehow, in that wreck, I lost my grip on Rostov's rifle. As it clattered away from me, a wave of fear crashed over me—without that gun, we were good as dead.

Rostov musta run outta bullets, 'cause his pistol fell silent. With his wing all banged up, I didn't reckon he would be able to reload. I was on my own, and any minute that gent up there was gonna realize the shooting stopped and make his move. I'd best have my paws around that rifle or he'd salt my hide.

Like a swarm of wasps, all of this sorta whizzed through my mind as I scrambled on my hands and knees after that rifle. Fear can be a mighty raw spur, and I reckon I was moving faster than I ever had in all my days. As my paws latched onto that rifle, I launched myself into a low dive.

Just as I dove, I heard the flat bark of a rifle and a bullet smacked the ground right where I'd been. Without hardly looking, much less aiming, I snapped a shot. My bullet barely made that bushwhacker blink, and in a heartbeat, he returned fire.

He'd hurried his shot and he missed. It was a close thing though. Close enough that I actually heard the bullet scream wickedly as it streaked past my head. Right then, I reckoned my best chance was to keep moving. Once I came up with that idea, you can bet I never let any grass grow under my feet. No, sir, I took off like a startled deer, covering the ground in giant bounds. As I ran, I could feel the prickly feeling of that bushwhacker's rifle follering me.

Just when I reckoned he had his sights locked on me, I dove, springing out like a man trying to fly. Even though I tried my best to fly, the notion never took. What I did was belly flop into a patch of tall grass.

I hit flat out and that fall jolted me like a mule kick, but I didn't let that trouble me any. I commenced to slithering through the grass like a spooked snake. I crawled a good forty yards before I had to stop.

The breath was whistling in and out of my mouth like a cyclone. As I glanced back at Rostov, it shocked me to see that in all of that confusion, I'd gotten a good two hundred yards closer to our attacker. Taking stock, I found that I was lying in the bottom of a small swell. I figured that for the moment I was safe. Even though his position was slightly above me, I didn't figure the bush-whacker could see me. In just a second, that feller proved me right, as he began to spray the tall grass with bullets. He never even came close to me. I guess I'd crawled a lot farther than he was allowing for.

Right then, I dearly would have loved to rest a mite, but I didn't dare. Any minute now, my friend up there was gonna get around to finishing Rostov off. I couldn't allow that to happen. I was the sheriff of these parts and it was my job to protect folks—even a sour-mouthed cuss like Rostov.

Now I got to thinking, a task that usually lands me eyebrow-deep in trouble, but I was doing it all the same. It came to me that since that gent didn't know exactly where I was, if I moved careful, I might be able to slip around behind him. I frowned down at the ground inches in front of my face. The only trouble was, it would take some time, and Rostov might not have a lot of time.

As I rassled with my problem, it dawned on me that it had gotten downright quiet. I raised my head and snuck a peek. Now, what did that sneaky bugger have on his mind? Then it walloped me upside the head. He was reloading.

I never even thought, I just powered up off the ground and charged. I was about halfway up to him when he popped his head up. I could see the shock wipe across his face as he saw me so close. Still galloping at a dead run, I fired and I missed. Screeching to a halt, I jacked the lever of that rifle and fired again. Or rather, I tried to fire. When I jerked the trigger, nothing happened. My rifle was bone-dry!

Ferrell didn't go down quietly. Clutching his leg and cursing wildly, he hit the ground hard. "You shot me, you lunkhead!" he screamed at Lester.

"Holy moly! I'm sorry," Lester screeched back, still backpedaling. He tangled his feet and tripped, falling heavily on the seat of his britches. "Jeez, mister, I'm sorry," he blubbered.

"Shut up!" Ferrell snapped, clutching his right calf where the bullet struck. "You shot me!" he repeated, still not believing it.

"I never meant to!" Lester screamed, wringing his hands.

Catrinia knelt, touching Ferrell's shoulder. "Are you all right?" she asked.

Still glaring at Lester, Ferrell only grunted, cursing his luck. They'd gotten away from Fedarov and his goons without hardly a scratch, and now to be downed by this simpleton! Out of the blue, it occurred to Ferrell that if Fedarov and his men were coming, that shot would draw them right here. As that thought raced through his mind, Ferrell pulled away from Catrinia, who was trying to stop the flow of blood from his leg. Pushing off with his good leg, Ferrell dove for the pistol Lester dropped. His dive came up a few feet short.

As he saw Ferrell going for the fallen pistol, Lester let out a squeal and scrambled for the gun himself. On two good legs, Lester was able to beat Ferrell by a hair. Snatching the pistol almost from under Ferrell's nose, he pointed it shakily with both hands. "Oh, no you don't," he shouted, scooting backward on his rear end. A sour expression on his face, he looked suspiciously at Ferrell. "You ain't hurt too bad," he said.

"I could travel," Ferrell agreed. "That shot will give away our position. If we want to hang onto our scalps, we better move."

Lester started shaking his head even before Ferrell finished talking. "We cain't move. Elmo wouldn't be able to find us. Besides, he said to stay right here."

Ferrell swore quickly and pounded his fist into the dirt. He was ready to argue, but Catrinia cut him off. "We can decide on that in a minute. First, we better do something to fix up your leg."

She helped Ferrell ease off his boot, then roll up his pant leg. She cringed back from the wound, her hand over her mouth. The bullet had ripped through the meaty part of the calf, tearing an ugly gashlike wound. "Oh, dear," Catrinia whispered. She looked from the wound up to Ferrell's face. "What do I do now?"

A grimace on his face, Ferrell leaned over to look at the wound. "That ain't so bad," he said, assessing the damage calmly. He took off his bandanna and passed it to Catrinia. "Tie this around it. It should be all right."

"I told you, you wasn't hurt bad," Lester said, climbing to his feet as Catrinia tied the bandanna around the wound. "Looks like a puny little scratch to me. I don't know why you was bellyaching for."

"You shot me, that's why!" Ferrell snapped.

"Well, if you ask me, you was asking for it!" Lester came back hotly.

"Asking for it?" Ferrell howled. "I was just standing there."

"Oh, yeah," Lester mumbled, his face falling as he recalled. "Well, I didn't like the way you was looking at me! I could tell you was scheming something."

"Maybe I was," Ferrell admitted, through clenched teeth. "But you kidnapped us. What do you expect?"

"Mr. Lester, I think we should get Ferrell into town. He should really have a doctor look at this."

Ferrell's heart skipped a beat, and a warm, rosy feeling spread through his body as he heard Catrinia use his first name, and the concern in her voice. She was worried about him.

Lester, on the other hand, had very little sympathy. "Aw, he ain't hurt none. I never seen so much cater-wauling over a such little scratch. Why, the way he's carrying on, you'd think he'd been gored by a steer or something."

Finished with her first aid, Catrinia rose gracefully to her feet. "Now, Lester, a man has been shot. I think you owe it to him to help."

"You're right about that," Lester agreed, a crafty look creeping across his face. "I'd say he needs some vittles.

A hurt man's gotta keep his strength up.'' Lester paused, practically beaming. ''Yes ma'am, I'd say a mess of vittles is what he needs to put him back right. I'll build a fire if you would stir something up.''

Catrinia laughed a little. ''Why, Lester, are you trying to tell me that you are hungry?'' she asked, a twinkle in her eye.

''You're darn tootin' I am!'' Lester said, smacking his lips. ''I'm hungry enough to eat a donkey saddle.''

Catrinia placed her hand on his shoulder and looked deep into his eyes. ''I am sorry to disappoint you, sir, but the truth is that I don't know how to cook.''

Both Ferrell and Lester jerked their heads up, Ferrell because he remembered how she promised to cook if he cleaned up that shack. Catrinia saw the glare; Ferrell headed her way. Instead of looking ashamed, she shot him a dazzling smile and a tiny shrug.

Lester, on the other hand, wasn't about to give up so easily. A truculent look on his face, he placed his hands on his hips and openly stared at Catrinia. ''Whatcha mean, you cain't cook?'' he demanded. ''You're a girly, ain't you?''

''Yes, but I never learned how to cook.''

''Never learnt!'' Lester howled, slapping the side of his face. ''I always reckoned womenfolk were born knowing how to whip up a meal.''

Catrinia smiled and shook her head. ''I'm afraid not. Even women have to learn how to cook, and I never did.''

"Not even a little bit?" Lester whimpered in a small voice. His face was still hopeful, but Catrinia crushed that hope when she shook her head. Lester's disappointment was so great that it almost buckled his knees. "What's the world comin' to?" he mumbled shaking his head. "I swear, who ever heard of a girl who didn't know how to cook?"

As Lester grumbled and stared at the ground, a cry sounded from the edge of the camp. As the trio turned to look, they saw Elmo stumble into the camp. Off balance, Elmo might have staggered plumb through the camp, but the rope around his neck twanged and cruelly jerked him to a halt.

A bemused smile on his face, Fedarov tossed the end of the rope to the dark-faced Yakov, then leaned forward on the saddle horn. "Good evening, Czaritsa. It is so good to see you again. I believe we have unfinished business."

Chapter Sixteen

Now, I always heard them Russians had a tendency to do things mighty straitlaced and formal like. I reckon that's why the bushwhacker done what he done. I mean, instead of just killing me, which he shoulda done, he stood real straight and tall. Moving deliberately, he brought the rifle up to his shoulder and sighted carefully down the barrel.

I reckon, to be polite I shoulda acted the same, but in Wyoming we do things a bit different. We jump right into a fight with both feet. We figure if you got some scrapping to do, you best pitch right in and get after it, then get about your business.

Well, the gist of it is, once I realized my rifle was empty and that gent had the drop on me, I didn't do any wasting around. I flung that rifle away and swooped for my pistol. I snatched her clean out of the holster and angled the business end right at him. Soon as I got that ol' hogleg lined up, I commenced to blasting, fanning the hammer like a crooked gambler raking in poker chips.

I'll say one thing for that Russian, he was tougher than a boardinghouse biscuit. Them slugs were knocking him right in the gullet and he held his ground. He finally got off his shot, but by that time he was swaying too much and missed by a mile.

Now, I hadn't really wanted to kill this feller, but he left me little choice in the matter. If he'd dropped his shooter and went down, I woulda stopped shooting. Instead, he braced his feet, his face pale and sweaty as he tried to cock his rifle.

When my pistol finally went dry, he was still on his feet. He was swaying like a tent pole in a tornado, but he was still up and trying. Just when I thought I was gonna have to go in and finish the job by hand, he took a little step forward, then nosed into the ground.

A sigh of relief whooshed past my lips. I hadn't been looking forward to piling into the man. Keeping an eye on him, I cracked open my shooter and plugged in some fresh shells. Once it was loaded, I rammed the pistol down in my holster and snatched onto Rostov's rifle. I didn't have any shells for it on me, so I just held it as I approached the dead man. Oh, he was dead all right, and it gave me no comfort to know I killed him. I figured he'd pretty much brought it on himself, but it still didn't rest easy on my mind.

Trying not to look at his face, I bent down and took his weapons. He didn't have a pistol, but he had a knife stuck in that red sash. Figuring that sash would make a good bandage for Rostov, I took it off. Poking the knife behind my belt, I carried the sash and both rifles down to Rostov.

That hardheaded Russian was still battling, trying to worm out from underneath that horse. When he saw me coming, he dropped his pistol and sagged back to the ground.

"You gonna make it?" I asked, dropping the rifles and kneeling down beside him.

"My wound is of no importance," he said stuffily. "We must get on the trail after Catrinia."

"I don't get that bleeding stopped, the only trail you're going down is the one that leads up to Saint Peter's house," I commented, thinking that Saint Peter might not answer the door when Rostov rang the bell.

Forgetting about that, I looked to his wound. Didn't look like much to me, the bullet had smashed through his upper shoulder. I picked him up a little and saw the bullet went clean through. I didn't see any bone flakes, so I figured it didn't do any more damage than tear up a little meat. Holding him in a sitting position, I tied that sash around the wounds, tying it tight so's to stop the bleeding.

That done, I spat in my hands, then set about to drag that horse off him. Now, I'm a mighty big man and stouter than most, but even I didn't have enough strength to budge that horse.

"Hang tight, I'll go find that feller's horse," I said, snapping my ruined boot off the ground and yanking it on my foot.

"I'm not going anywhere," Rostov said dryly. I had to stop and peer back over my shoulder to make sure it was Rostov who was talking and not that dead horse. I mean, he almost made a joke and that didn't sound like Rostov. Of the two of them, I figured that horse had the better sense of humor. Well, it mighta been the horse, 'cause Rostov sure wasn't smiling.

Limping along on my holed-up boot, I had to do some prowling and hunting, but I finally spied the dead man's horse. I done some looking for my own horse, but the stupid critter was nowhere to be found. I reckoned the miserable beast was already bellied up to the trough back at Burdett's stable.

Grumbling about my dumb horse, my ruined boot, and the state of things in general, I led that horse down to Rostov. With the horse doing most of the work, we skidded Rostov's dead horse off his leg. That Russian bounced right to his feet, but he never stayed there. First time he put weight on that bum leg, he went down like a sack of horse apples.

Now, so help me, I didn't mean to do 'er, but I had to laugh. He sure looked funny flopping to the ground thataway. Rostov sure never saw the humor in it, but then I reckon he wouldn't see the humor in a cow chip fight. Rumbling like a wagon with a busted wheel, he glared up at me. "Would you please assist me in getting up? My leg is numb."

Still grinning, I hauled the big devil up to his feet. He stood on his good leg, shaking the other like a man with ants in his drawers. Well, let me tell you, when the blood went to trickling down that leg again, his eyes shot wide open. I swear, his face turned three different colors.

Finally, without a word, he turned and limped up to the man I shot. Smirking to myself, I carried the rifles and led the horse after him. "That's Pavel!" he stammered when he saw the body.

"Yeah, what of it?" I said.

A thoughtful expression stamped on his wide face, Rostov glanced from the body up to me. "Pavel was the finest shot in all of Russia."

I really didn't know what to say to that, so I just shrugged and said, "This ain't Russia."

Rostov shook his head slowly. "I do not understand. I saw him aim at you. Pavel has never been known to miss. How is it that you still live?"

I hauled out my old pistol and gave her a twirl, something I'd been practicing. "Your man was too slow," I said, showing him the pistol, then ramming it back down in the holster. "Your man had the drop on me all right, but he took his time and never got off a shot. While he was busy aiming, I fetched out my old hogleg and drilled him."

"You would have to do that very quickly," Rostov observed, rubbing his chin. "And to still score a hit, that is amazing."

Well, sir, I swelled up like a peach floating in a water barrel. I hooked my thumbs in my belt, all set to tell him how I done it. All of a sudden, it hit me. I was all puffed up about killing a man, and that wasn't right. Feeling plumb ashamed, I turned my back and shrugged. "He left me little choice. I just done what I had to do," I said simply.

When I turned back, Rostov was beside the body, going through the dead man's pockets. "What are you doing?" I barked, remembering him razzing me earlier. "Surely you Russians do not rob the dead?"

I swear, that Russian had the sense of humor of a lava rock. Or maybe he didn't think it was proper to be making a joke with a dead man lying at your feet. I didn't mean no disrespect, I was just feeling a little low and figured a joke would help. Either way, Rostov never laughed, never even cracked a smile. A high and mighty expression stamped on his face, he glared back over his shoulder at me. "No," he growled as he stuffed the man's stuff into his own pockets. "I served with this man for many years. He was a friend, I knew his family well. I merely wish to return these things to them."

"You sound as if you're sorry he's dead. In case it slipped your mind, that jasper was trying to smoke us and he liked to got the job done."

Grimacing as he moved, Rostov straightened up. I could tell that leg was paining him, and I reckon he dearly wanted to rub it, but he never done it. Instead he went to running his jaw. "I have not forgotten what Pavel done," he said haughtily. "This was not Pavel's fault."

"Not his fault!" I howled, slapping the side of my

face. "You forgetting that he was the one slinging the lead at us?"

"I do not blame Pavel. He was merely following orders. I blame Boris Fedarov for this!" At the end, Rostov's voice grew angry and he was chomping his jaws like a toothless man eating roastin' ears.

"Now, hold on a minute," I protested. "Maybe this gent Fedaroof was the kingpin, but this polecat was the one working that rifle. I reckon he's as much to blame as anybody."

"No," Rostov replied quietly and shook his head. "Pavel was a good man. Fedarov was his superior, and Pavel was merely following the orders of a superior, like a good Russian."

Now, I didn't like the sound of that. The last thing I wanted to hear was that the man I just killed was a good family man. Anyway, Rostov's words didn't make any sense to me, and I was in the mood to argue a mite. "You're trying to tell me that just because this Fedaroof told him to do it, that this man was right for bushwhacking us?"

"A good Russian always follows orders. That way, we have order and harmony. Not the chaos I see in your country."

I bulled right up to him, my neck plumb hot. "You best slap a hackamore on that tongue, Ruskie. Nobody talks bad about my country. America is the best place in the world," I sputtered, jabbing a finger at him. "If you ask me, this man is just as guilty as Fedaroof," I declared, pointing down at the dead man. "If he didn't like the orders Fedaroof gave him, he shoulda told the bugger to go play with a meadow muffin."

I don't reckon I convinced Rostov, but he didn't put up a scrap. Instead, he clapped me on the shoulder, and danged if he didn't almost smile. "I can see you feel guilty about shooting Pavel, and you wish to ease your mind by saying he was a bad man, but this is just not true." Rostov gave my shoulder a tiny squeeze. "Do not worry. I do not blame you. As you said, you did what you had to do, as did Pavel. Such are the fortunes of men. Do not let it trouble you further."

"It ain't troubling me. I kilt fellers before," I declared hotly and twisted away from that big Russian. I placed my hands on my hips and glared at him. "And if any more of your buddies wander in front of my sights, I'll send them down the same trail as this feller."

With that, I sat down and tugged the boots off the dead man. I figured, since he blasted a hole in mine, it was only fair that I have his. It didn't work thataway, though. That Pavel gent had feet like a sparrow. I couldn't hardly get my big toe in his pint-size cloppers. Throwing them away in disgust, I jerked on my own boots and got ready to move out.

Since my horse was long gone and Rostov's was dead, we only had Pavel's mount. Now, I'd just as soon take a castor oil elixir as walk, but I gave that horse to Rostov. I knew the big Russian's leg wouldn't carry him out of sight and we had a long way to go.

I confiscated Pavel's rifle for myself and gave Rostov's weapon back to him. ''Thanks for the loan. It came in right handy,'' I grumbled as I passed it over to him.

Now, in all the excitement, I'm sure you can see how a feller might forget to go back and reload. No, sir, I didn't really think that Rostov carrying an empty rifle was my fault, but try and tell that to that hardheaded Russian.

Whoever's fault it was, we were soon to regret not tamping that rifle plumb full of bullets—dearly regret it.

Chapter Seventeen

Her eyes wide and watching Fedarov closely, Catrinia inched closer to Ferrell. Ferrell had warned this could happen, but she hadn't really believed it. Ferrell had hurt them badly back in the cabin. Catrinia would never have believed Fedarov and his men could recover and come after them so quickly, but here they were. Even big Yuri, limping and with a rag tied around his broken jaw. Holding a hand to the jaw, he glared at Ferrell with open hate.

"Did you really think that you could escape us, Duchess?" Fedarov asked, then calmly handed his reins to Yakov and swung down from his horse. "Now, perhaps, we can finish our business."

Lester finally remembered he was holding a pistol. His hands trembling, he guided the weapon at Fedarov. "Just hold onto your drawers, string bean!" he shouted.

Disdain stamped on his face, Fedarov coldly stared at Lester. "Do you wish to shoot me?" he asked, pulling the soft leather gloves from his fingers. "If that is your wish, then, please, fire."

"You best not push me, scarecrow. I ain't spoofin'," Lester declared. "I done winged that jasper," he added, waving the pistol at Ferrell.

"Oh, I believe you," Fedarov said, bending down beside the fire and pouring himself a cup of coffee. He smiled over the rim of the cup at Lester. "As I said, you may shoot me if you so desire, but the act will certainly cost you your life, to say nothing of a fortune."

"Fortune?" both Lester and Elmo whispered, their ears pricking. "Whadda you mean, fortune?" Lester asked with keen interest.

Fedarov smiled and tasted the coffee. He lowered the cup, wrinkling his nose in disgust. "I'll never see why you Americans are so fond of coffee. I prefer tea myself." He took another small taste, then threw the cup carelessly on the ground. "Perhaps we can help each other."

"What you yapping about?" Elmo demanded fiercely.

"You and your brother wish to ransom the duchess for money. That is correct?"

"You better believe it, buster!" Elmo sputtered, throwing the rope from around his neck. "And if you know what's good for you, you and your pals won't get in our road."

Fedarov smiled and spread his hands. "We have no intentions of standing in your way," he said, his smile growing as he slapped his gloves into his hand. "In fact, we wish to help you."

"Help us?" Elmo howled, rubbing his raw neck. "You sure got a funny way of helping."

"I am sorry if we were a bit rough earlier, but we

could not afford to take any chances.'' Ignoring the pistol in Lester's fist, Fedarov stepped between the two brothers, putting his arms over their shoulders. ''Our mission is too important for us to take any chances, especially with men like you, who are obviously fighters.'' By now, Fedarov's voice was booming like a soapbox preacher, and his words were having an affect. Already Elmo and Lester looked happy. ''But now that we know you are on our side, we can strike a deal. You want money and we wish to block the sale of Alaska from our country to yours. Our two goals coincide.''

Lester and Elmo exchanged blank looks as Lester scratched the side of his face with the pistol. ''Is he talking English? ''I didn't savvy a word he said.''

''Me neither,'' Elmo put in.

Fedarov mostly managed to cover the irritation that flickered across his face. ''What I'm saying is that we wish your help. We want you to deliver a message to the proper authorities in Whiskey City.''

''What kind of message?'' Elmo demanded.

''About your money, of course,'' Fedarov said, pulling a pencil and piece of paper from his pocket. ''How much money were you thinking of asking for?''

''Ten thousand dollars,'' Lester replied proudly.

''Ten thousand dollars,'' Fedarov echoed, stepping over beside Catrinia. Holding the paper and pencil in his left hand, he ran the back of his right hand over her cheek. ''For the daughter of Alexander? Such a figure is an insult. Her creamy skin is worth ten times that amount. How does one hundred thousand dollars sound to you?''

''A hunert thousand dollars,'' Lester marveled as he tried to calculate how much money that was. His mind wasn't near up to the task and threw a spoke. He staggered back like he'd been whiffed by a cedar post. ''Jezabel,'' he muttered and fell flat on his backside.

Elmo wore a similar dazed expression, but he managed to keep his feet. ''Why, it'd take a wagon to haul that much money.''

''Perhaps,'' Fedarov replied, managing a tolerant smile. ''I trust you gentlemen wouldn't have a problem with such an encumbrance?''

Elmo wasn't right sure what the fancy Russian said, and he didn't care. He wanted the money. He licked his lips. ''What do we have to do?''

Fedarov held out the pencil and paper to the two brothers. ''Simply write a ransom note and take it to Whiskey City.''

Lester and Elmo stared at the paper, but neither of them made a move to take it from Fedarov. ''Cain't read nor write,'' Lester explained.

''Neither of you can read nor write?'' Fedarov asked, a look of amazement on his face.

Elmo sucked in a long, sniffling breath. ''Don't need to,'' he said, slapping his empty holster. ''We prefer to do our talking with a six-gun.''

Fedarov quickly wrote the ransom note. He folded the note carefully, then held it out. ''All you have to do is deliver this note to the proper authorities in Whiskey City. You'll probably have to hang around for a few days, but once they get the money together, bring it back here.''

"Don't do it," Catrinia pleaded. "If it's money you want, I'll pay you all you want to help us get to Whiskey City."

"Shut up," Fedarov snapped as Lester looked uncertainly at the gun still clutched in his hand. Fedarov drew back his hand to strike Catrinia, but held it just in time. "You speak rashly, my lady. By this time next week, your family won't have enough money to buy a moldy loaf of bread."

Fedarov snapped his hand down, pointing a long finger at Lester and Elmo, who both stumbled back a step. "You two, you want the money?" he asked, and after exchanging a long glance, they both nodded slowly. He passed Elmo his pistol. "Then get going."

"Yes, sir," they both said and hurried to their horses.

The dark, morose Yakov watched them go. When they were out of earshot, Yakov turned to his boss. "Are you sure we can trust these two, Boris Fedarov?"

"I trust their greed," Fedarov said with a shrug. "It is imperative that the ransom note be delivered by an American. Any Russian involvement in the duchess's disappearance must be concealed."

"As I understand," Yakov agreed. "But it is foolish to trust such an important task to those simpletons. We need that money, if the rest of our plan is to succeed."

Fedarov listened to Yakov and turned the gloves in his hands. "They are an inept pair," he agreed, his gaze traveling over the three men left in his force. Fedarov wanted Yakov with him and Yuri was in no shape to travel, so that left Vladamir. A solid man who followed orders without question, Vladamir was a man who needed orders to follow. On his own, Vladamir was lost.

Still, Fedarov had very little choice. Pavel was not back, and Vladamir was all Boris had. Boris Fedarov cocked a finger at Vladamir. "Vladamir, I have a task for you."

"Yes, sir," Vladamir said, snapping to attention.

"I want you to follow those two. Do not let them see you. If they mess up, kill them and deliver the note to Dmitri and Vanya. They should be in Whiskey City by now. They will know what to do with it. Do you understand your orders?"

"Yes, sir," Vladamir said, saluting crisply. Doing a smart about-face, Vladamir marched stiffly to his horse. As darkness slowly closed in around him Vladamir rode after the two brothers.

Even though Fedarov gave his orders in Russian, Ferrell knew what he said, as Catrinia whispered a hurried translation. Ferrell sighed, looking at Catrinia. They both knew they could expect no help from Lester and Elmo. The brothers were as good as dead. Between the two of them, they couldn't do anything right, not even if their lives depended on it—which this time they did.

Fedarov glanced at his two captives. "Do not mourn for them. You shall not live to see their deaths."

*   *   *

I ain't a natural walker to begin with, and now I was having more trouble than usual. I don't know if you ever tried walking with a big hole blasted in your boot, but take it from me, it ain't easy.

To make matters worse, I kept looking up at Rostov, perched in the saddle, comfortable as you please. I was nowhere near happy; then Rostov open his yap and I durn near blew my top. "I shall miss Pavel."

"I don't know why," I grumbled. "He tried to punch your ticket and in case you forgot, he like to got the job done."

Rostov shrugged. "Pavel was merely following orders. Had he killed me, he would have felt bad, as I feel for him."

"You Ruskies sure got a peculiar way of treating your friends. I mean even if the president hisself told me to do it, I wouldn't snuff one of my friends. I'd tell the president to go get stuffed."

"You could not talk to your leader that way," Rostov protested, his voice stern.

"Why not?" I asked, shrugging. "I mean, the president is just a man. He ain't no better than the rest of us. And neither is your czar."

Arkady Rostov's face was grave as he glared down at me. "Since you have done myself and my country a great service, I shall overlook your hasty remarks. In the future, I caution you to guard your tongue. In my country, you could receive twenty lashes for speaking against the czar."

"Well, we ain't in your country. Out here, we say what we got on our minds," I informed him. "And another thing, if I ever run across this czar of yours, I plan to give him a piece of my mind," I blustered.

Now I was shootin' off my mouth. Although I meant what I said, I didn't figure to ever bump into the czar, so I blustered some. I don't know why, but I was building a powerful dislike for that czar. He sounded like a pushy stuffed shirt to me, and that rubbed my fur wrong.

To my surprise, Rostov laughed. It liked to shocked me outta my socks. I never heard him laugh before. I know I woulda remembered, 'cause his laugh rumbled like a rock slide.

"You are a most stubborn man," Rostov boomed heartily. "What is the expression you Americans use? Hardheaded?"

Hardheaded! Me? I stopped dead still, placing my hands on my hips as I glared up at him. Call me hardheaded, would he? That was a hoot, coming from a hombre that had a pumpkin like a granite boulder.

I was sucking up a full charge of wind to really let him have it, when Rostov laughed again. "Do not be offended, my friend. I know I am the same," he said, then shrugged. "Perhaps it is the way of men?"

He kinda snatched the wind from my sails, and before I could conjure myself up a comeback, he offered his hand down to me. "Climb aboard, my friend. We will make better time if we both ride."

"We'll ride that horse into the ground," I protested.

"Does it matter? At our present rate of speed, we will never reach Catrinia in time. We must hurry."

He had a point and I was fed up with walking, so I took his hand and swung up behind him. Rostov kicked the horse into motion, and we set out at a good clip. Me and Rostov are both big men, but that horse carried us for several hours. It was pitch dark when the pony stumbled the first time.

"I guess we walk from here," I said. That horse had given us all he could, and I didn't see the need in killing him for a few more miles.

Rostov must have felt the same, because he dropped the reins and eased himself down. A grave expression on his face, he held out his hand to me. "You do not need to go on. I know you are tired and you have already done enough. You stay and rest. I shall go on alone."

Now, my shoulders felt like I had a gorilla on my back, and I was ready to cave in, but I'd be hanged if I was gonna let that contrary Ruskie outdo me. I slapped his hand out of the way and took off walking. "I signed on for the full hitch. You just make sure you keep up," I said, growling as I went past him.

We set out walking with that horse follering headdown behind us. I gotta say, for a man with a bruised leg and a shot shoulder, Rostov kept up pretty good. 'Course, by now, my foot was sore as a boil, and that slowed me some.

Even though we were walking, the night air was cold as the south end of a brass monkey. I started to shiver a mite, when Rostov pressed something into my hand. It took several minutes to figure out what it was, and when I did, my heart jumped. A whiskey flask! I didn't need nobody to tell me what to do with that. I pried it open and took a quick jolt.

"That is vodka. A favorite drink in my country," Rostov said as I handed the flask back to him.

Now, I never heard of vodka before, but I took to it like money from home. As the warmth spread through my body, I felt a surge of energy. Rostov had himself a snort and he musta got the same kick in the pants, 'cause before I knew it, we were hitching along at a fair pace.

Walking and nipping at that hooch jug, we covered some miles. Finally, we stove plumb up and collapsed to the ground. As I lay on the ground, I saw Rostov sitting, just staring at the empty silver flask.

"Catrinia gave me this two years ago for my birthday." Rostov ran a big hand under his nose and stared at me with haunted eyes. "And now, I have failed her!"

"You done your best," I told him.

"No!" Rostov roared, surging to his feet. "I shall not rest until she is safe!"

I guess all his blubbering got to me, or else I just didn't want to admit that some greenhorn foreigner could outdo me. Either way, I climbed to my feet. Mad and determined, we set out again.

Our anger carried us a half mile, then began to drain away. It takes a pile of energy to stay mad and when you are dead-dog tired, you can't do 'er. I was ready to fold my tent and cave in right there. I reckon Rostov felt the same; he looked ready to drop. Then we heard it— the sound of sobbing up ahead. Me and Rostov stared at each other. We had found her!

Chapter Eighteen

Me and Rostov spent ten minutes sneaking up on that sobbing sound. When we finally got close, we still couldn't see much, so we just threw caution to the wind and rushed in. Well, to be downright truthful, we didn't exactly rush in, we were too sore for that. We hobbled in like a couple of three-legged dogs.

What we found wasn't Rostov's duchess, but Stevie and Jenny Hunt. They were huddled together, crying and sniffling like a couple of lost puppies.

When he saw us, Stevie stood up, hurriedly trying to wipe the tears from his eyes. "Teddy, am I glad to see you," he said, trying to maintain a little dignity.

Jenny, on the other hand, didn't give a hoot 'bout dignity. "Teddy!" she cried, rushing over and hugging my leg. A second later, Stevie done the same thing.

I didn't know what to do. I just stood there with a kid grafted onto each hip. "What the devil are you kids doing way out here?" I asked, trying to pry them loose.

Finally, Stevie let go. He backed off, looking me

square in the eye. "We were out looking for Princess Catrinia."

"Why in the devil would you do that?" I asked.

"Well, I knew where they were hiding her, and we figured—"

Before Stevie could finish, Rostov cut him off with a mighty roar. "You know where Catrinia is?"

Stevie hung his head. "I thought I did. I heard them talking when they took her off the stage, but I guess I got lost, 'cause we couldn't find the cabin."

"They're holding her at a cabin?" I asked, and Stevie nodded. I shot a quick look at Rostov. "There's only one cabin out here. I know where it is. It's real close!"

"You children, do you have horses?" he asked, and Stevie nodded.

Well, sir, we bundled them kids up and loaded on their horses. Rostov held Jenny, and Stevie rode behind me. In twenty minutes, we were looking down at that cabin. The place was dark as a tomb at midnight and there didn't seem to be any movement.

"I do not see any horses in the corral," Rostov whispered. "Perhaps this is not the place."

"It has to be," I insisted. "There ain't another cabin for miles. Maybe they staked their horses out to graze. Let's go check it out." I eased my rifle from the boot, then handed my reins to Stevie. "I want you and Jenny to stay here and guard the horses. I'm giving you an important job, so don't let me down. We'll signal you when it's safe to come down."

Stevie nodded gravely at me and I gave his leg a little squeeze on the knee. Rostov had already started down, and I hurried to catch him. Carrying our rifles ready, we crossed the dark yard in silence. We took positions on either side of the door.

"Ready?" Rostov whispered, his hand on the doorknob.

I took a deep breath, then nodded. Rostov threw that door open, and I leaped inside, my eyes sweeping across the cabin. I saw the figure of a man curled up in the corner. Jumping across the room in two bounds, I jabbed him in the gizzard with my rifle. "Don't move!" I screeched at the top of my lungs.

Rostov had rushed in behind me, and seeing no one else in the cabin, he lit a match. As the tiny yellow light made a small dent in the darkness, I jabbed the man again with my rifle. "All right, get up," I barked.

I stepped back, but the feller never moved. My patience already thin as hotel soup, I toed him none too gently with my boot. "Get up, or I'll whup the tar outta you!" I squawked.

The man still didn't move, and as I stepped up to apply a little persuasion, Rostov found a lamp and lit it. As the light spread through the room, I realized there was something odd about this man. I bent a little closer.

"Yeow!" I yelped, springing back. "He's dead!" I squawked, shivering a little.

"Ivan!" Rostov exclaimed.

"One of yourn?" I asked, but I didn't need to. I'd already seen the red sash around his waist.

"Yes, he was one of my men," Rostov answered absently, his eyes busy circling the room. "Catrinia is not here."

"No, but I reckon she was," I said, pointing to the mop bucket. "They done some cleaning. I reckon she was behind that."

Rostov nodded and looked ready to say something else, but we heard a scrape from outside. Whirling together, we trained our rifles on the door, ready for whatever might come in.

"Don't shoot, it's us," I heard Stevie call. "Is it safe to come in?"

"Yeah, come on in," I said, mighty annoyed "Dad burn it, boy, I thought I told you to stay put."

"No, you said to guard the horses and come down when it was safe," Stevie corrected. "Besides, Jenny was cold."

I done some growling and cussing under my breath. One of these days, somebody was gonna have to learn that boy to listen and obey. I figured it'd have to be me, but I didn't want to tackle the chore right then.

As Rostov started a fire, I took the lantern and went outside. Holding the lamp close to the ground, I scouted for tracks. What I found was two sets of tracks that took out lickety-split, and three or four riders that followed at a slower pace.

"I reckon one of them helped her and she got away," I told Rostov as I came back inside. "Not that she is going to stay away. The way she was running that horse, it'll give out on her, then they'll nab her again. First light, we better go after her.''

Rostov rubbed his chin, then nodded his head at the light. ''With the lamp, could we go now?''

''I suppose we could stick with the trail, as long as they keep running them horses, anyway,'' I replied slowly, then pointed to Stevie and Jenny. ''What about them?''

''I found supplies in a sack over there on the table. There is plenty of wood for the fire. They could stay here.''

''Could you do that?'' I asked Stevie. ''Could you stay here and take care of your sister?''

''Yes, sir, but I'd rather go with you.''

I knelt down, putting my arm on Stevie's shoulder. ''No, son, your place is here with your sister. We'll be back before night, or sometime in the morning at the latest. I don't want you to leave this cabin. You hear me?'' I asked, and he nodded gravely.

I didn't feel at all right about leaving them, but I didn't know what else to do. This might be our last chance of finding that duchess. I figured if we didn't catch up with them by nightfall tonight, I'd leave the chase to Rostov and turn back.

We said our good-byes, and Rostov told the kids how proud of them he was. He gave them a whole spiel about what a service they did for Russia; meanwhile I cooled my heels in the doorway. It was an hour short of sunup when we finally set out, the night crisp and still.

* * *

A little afraid of Fedarov and wanting the money he promised, Lester and Elmo rode hard. As the distance between them and Fedarov widened, they slowly relaxed and slowed down. "A hunnert thousand dollars," Lester commented wonderingly. "How much jack is that anyway?"

"Elmo scratched his chin and looked up at the dark sky. "A pile. I reckon we'll be the richest two gents in the whole world."

"Wow! Imagine that," Lester said, his head whirling with thoughts of all the things he could buy.

After a few more miles, the excitement began to wear off, and the loss of a night's sleep began to catch up with the brothers.

"To heck with that sourpuss Fedarov, let's stop. Whiskey City will still be there whenever we make it," Elmo suggested.

Always ready to eat or sleep, Lester was already stopped and off his horse before Elmo finished talking. As they stripped the saddles from their horses, Lester stopped working and leaned against his horse. "Elmo, I don't want to go into Whiskey City. I'm afraid they'll hang us."

'Aw, they'll forgive and forget. Besides, they can't kill us, not as long as we are the only ones that know where the princess is."

"I been thinking on that," Lester said, getting around to what was really bothering him. "I kinda liked her."

"Yeah. She was kinda flighty, giggling all the time, but I sorta took to her myself," Elmo agreed.

"You think he'd hurt her?" Lester asked.

Elmo nodded. "I been thinking on that. I don't reckon that Fedarov figures on letting her go."

Lester didn't say anything as they finished tending their horses in silence. They didn't notice the shadowy figure slip up to the edge of their camp, watching them.

Vladamir watched the two brothers unsaddle their horses and make camp. Once he was sure they were turning in for the night, he pulled back. About fifty yards from their camp, Vladamir found a place of his own. He tended his own horse, then seated himself on a fallen tree, watching the winking light of their fire.

They made a fire, but for once, even Lester wasn't hungry. He spread his blanket and laid down, watching as Elmo struggled to pull off his boots. "You know, Elmo, I don't feel right about this whole deal."

"Me neither," Elmo admitted, fingering the raw rope burn around his neck. "But that Fedarov is a mighty rough customer. He ain't gonna like us letting him down."

"He don't scare me none," Lester said, but he was lying. "All of a sudden, I don't even want the money. I would feel better if we was helping that girl."

"A man could get a sprung back totin' around that much money," Elmo agreed solemnly. "Besides, I owe that polecat for roping me. I say we go back and fix his little wagon."

"You think we could?" Lester worried. "That's three mighty salty men."

"'Course we could handle them! We..." Elmo stopped and swallowed the sudden lump in his throat. "I mean, if we snuck up on them and opened up 'fore they knew we was about."

"Yeah, maybe we could catch them snoozing."

"We'd have to leave right now to make it back there before morning," Elmo said.

"I ain't tired no more," Lester said.

They looked at each other for a long time, then without a word, they jumped out of their beds. "That lady said she would pay us for helping her," Elmo said as they rolled their beds.

Lester straightened up, a grin breaking across his face. "We're gonna be rich after all."

All smiles again, the brothers quickly broke camp and saddled their horses. Neither spoke as they backtracked toward Fedarov's camp. They rode within ten yards of Vladamir, who had fallen asleep and never even saw them.

A few seconds later, Vladamir woke, some small noise of their passage alerting him. The first thing he did was glance lazily down at their camp. It took his sleepy mind a few seconds to realize that the fire was out. With a shock, Vladamir realized he'd been duped!

Jumping to his feet, he rushed through the darkness, running down to the camp. Once he was sure they had gone, Vladamir set down on the ground and tried to think.

He didn't want to go back and tell Boris Fedarov that he had failed, but Vladamir didn't know what else to do.

It never occurred to him to simply ride away and disappear. Vladamir had been following orders his whole life. Without them, he was lost.

Finally, he decided he must report this to Boris, but Vladamir didn't get in any hurry. Moving at the slowest possible speed, he saddled his horse and set out.

Lester and Elmo had good intentions. They rode hard, intent on carrying out their self-appointed mission of saving the princess.

"How much you reckon they'll give us fer pulling that princess's fat outta the fire?" Lester wondered, neither him nor Elmo noticing that in the dark they had veered off course.

"It'd be a good pile. I s'pect they'll want to knight us and give us one of them fancy tin suits."

"No kiddin'?" Lester replied, rubbing his jaw. "I reckon I'd like that."

Lester and Elmo discussed what they would buy and do, until the sun beginning to poke over the horizon caught their attention. Stupefied expressions on their long faces, the two brothers gaped at each other.

"That the sun a-comin' up?" Lester asked, rising in the saddle to scratch his backside. "Cain't be the sun. If this were sunup, we'd already be back at the camp."

They stared at each other, then it finally hit them. They'd gotten lost and ridden right by Fedarov's camp!

Chapter Nineteen

After Vladamir had gone, Fedarov turned to Catrinia and Ferrell. "I suggest that both of you enjoy this night and tomorrow's sunrise. They will be the last you ever see."

Catrinia didn't respond; all she did was catch her breath and squeeze Ferrell's hand. As he felt her hand on his, Ferrell wanted to jump up and smash Fedarov's head in. Knowing he would be killed before he got off the ground, Ferrell bit his lips and bided his time. Now was not the time for anything rash. Fedarov had given them until morning. Ferrell could only hope the Russians would let their guard down during the night.

Fedarov frowned at this lack of response to his threats. He started to say something, then abruptly turned away. He stalked over to the horses, taking a sheaf of paper from his saddlebag. "Your stationery, my lady," he said, holding the paper up for her to see.

Fedarov glanced at the paper, then dropped it at Catrinia's feet. "I want you to start writing. Write several letters to your father. Tell him what a wonderful time you're having and how grand it is here. Tell him, he should come personally for the signing of the Alaska treaty.''

For a second, Catrinia's fear was pushed to the back of her mind as curiosity took over. ''But why?'' she wanted to know. ''Why would you want my father to come to America? You said you wished to block the sale of Alaska.''

''That was for those two dupes,'' Fedarov replied with a shrug. ''Surely, you do not think that I would trust the truth about our plans to them?''

''What is so important about my father coming here?''

''In Russia, your father is well protected. Only family members and trusted advisors can get close to him. But here,'' Fedarov said, sweeping his arm wide. ''Here, in this barbaric place, they allow the most common of men to get close to their leaders. Also, there are men who would kill for the right price.'' Fedarov smiled down at Catrinia. ''We plan to hire these men to assassinate your father!''

''Why? Because you do not possess the courage to do it yourself?'' Catrinia flared, using anger to check her fear and hold back the tears.

Fedarov laced his fingers together and began to pace. ''No, we do not fear your father, but after he is gone, we wish to ascend to power ourselves.'' Fedarov stopped, his face practically glowing. He enjoyed telling how brilliant he and his comrades had been. ''Many in Russia still worship the czar, they would never allow us to seize power if it were known that we had him killed. So we will have these wild Americans do it for us. After his death, we shall express our sorrow, and in our country's darkest hour, we shall put aside our grief and step in to run things. History shall remember us as heroes!''

''You're mad,'' Catrinia whispered, the horror she felt sounding in her voice. ''You cannot take power. It shall fall to my brother Nicholas.''

''If he still lives. We hope he shall accompany your father.'' Fedarov shrugged. ''If not, we have other plans.''

Catrinia wanted to say something, But Ferrell beat her to it. ''Why kidnap Catrinia? Once her father hears of it, your whole deal will be blown.''

''We needed the money,'' Fedarov answered, then smirked down at Catrinia. ''In a way, you shall pay for the destruction of your own father. But don't get your hopes up. Your father shall not hear of your fate. Any messages to him about this shall be intercepted.''

''Who's gonna pay the money then?'' Ferrell asked.

Fedarov smiled. ''Why, your own American government, of course. You Americans are so generous. Your government will be happy to pay.''

''They'll not just fork over the money and forget about it. They'll want to see Catrinia afterward,'' Ferrell countered.

''Of course they will,'' Fedarov boomed. ''We have a young lady who looks remarkably similar to the duchess. My men and I will catch the bandits, you and those two brothers. You will be killed in the battle, and alas the money shall never be found, but the duchess will be safe. Our Catrinia shall graciously thank the American people for everything they have done.'' Fedarov patted Catrinia on the head. ''She will finish your tour for you, mailing the letters you shall write along the way. Your letters shall convince your father to attend the formal signing this fall.'' His face turning harsh, Fedarov squatted in front of Catrinia. ''You can die knowing you and your father shall both be buried in this same, godforsaken continent. Now, Czaritsa, please, write the letters.''

Catrinia showed her regal heritage as her head came up and she looked Fedarov square in the eye. ''You're mad if you think I would help you lure my father to his own death,'' she said, her tone icy. She gave him an aloof stare and crossed her arms over her chest. ''And since you have already said you plan to kill me, you cannot force me to write them.''

''Can't we, Czaritsa?'' Fedarov asked softly, then slapped her. ''Write the letters!''

At the sound of the slap, Ferrell started to spring to his feet, but Yakov's rifle suddenly at his throat held him back. Her eyes still glued to Fedarov, Catrinia touched Ferrell's shoulder. ''It is all right, Ferrell,'' she said coolly. She kept her head up and refused to touch the trickle of blood coming from the corner of her mouth.

''Perhaps you do not fully appreciate your situation, Czaritsa?'' Fedarov said, using the respectful title sarcastically. "We need only your right hand. Yakov is very good with a knife. He could start by cutting off your toes, then your feet. Or what of your friend? We could shoot his kneecaps. Are you prepared to listen to his screams all night? Or your own?"

Horror stamped on her face, Catrinia reached a trembling hand for the paper. Hesitating, she looked back at Ferrell. "Go ahead," he said gently.

Tears streaming down her face, Catrinia started to write. Fedarov didn't move until she finished the first letter. He snatched it from her hand, reading quickly. "That will do, but try and sound more cheerful. After all, you are having a good time. Now write some more," he told her, then turned to his two men. "Keep a watch on them. I am going to sleep."

As Fedarov lay down and went to sleep, Ferrell began to hope. Maybe the other two would nod off. Watching them closely, Ferrell put his arm around Catrinia, holding her close as she wrote.

As the night wore on, Ferrell never took his eyes off the two Russians. Even though tomorrow might be his last day on earth, sitting with his arm around Catrinia, Ferrell could not help but feel a small sense of bliss.

Finally, Yakov's head slumped to his chest, and he began to snore softly. Ferrell shifted his eyes to Yuri, but the big man was still awake, glaring across the fire at Ferrell. Ferrell wished he hadn't hit the big man so hard. With his broken jaw, Yuri was in too much misery to sleep. He simply sat with his rifle across his knees, one hand holding his jaw.

Ferrell felt Catrinia's whole body jerk as a sob escaped past her lips. "Don't worry, I'll get us out of this." Ferrell made the promise, knowing it was likely an empty one.

"I feel like I'm betraying my father."

"I know, but right now we have a chance. Had you resisted, they would have shot our knees and we would be helpless," Ferrell told her, stroking her hair and wiping the tears from her face. "Can they really keep your father from finding out about all of this?"

"Maybe," Catrinia admitted. "A man named Misha Cherlanko screens all of my father's correspondences. If he is on their side, he could hold back any message of this."

"Keep writing," Ferrell said, not knowing what else to do. He wished Yuri was closer. Maybe then, he might have a chance to jump the big Russian. But the way things were now, Yuri could shoot him ten times before Ferrell could cover half the distance between them.

As a pinkish glow began to grow in the eastern sky, a desperation crept up on Ferrell. It would be daylight soon, and he could afford to wait no longer. He had to do something before Yakov and Fedarov woke up.

Moving slowly, Ferrell took his arm from Catrinia's shoulder. "Don't move. I'm going to get us out of this," he whispered as he drew his feet underneath him. The place where Lester shot him was stiff and very sore, but Ferrell hoped the leg would take his weight. If it wouldn't, he and Catrinia were both dead.

Across the camp, Yuri saw Ferrell's furtive movements and heard the whispering. He couldn't make out the words, and in English, he would not have understood them anyway. Yuri didn't have to hear the words to know what was going on. The American was going to make his try.

Had his jaw not been throbbing so terribly, Yuri would have smiled. This was what he had been waiting for all night. Yuri owned Ferrell, and now came the payback. Yuri had it all worked out in his mind. He would let the American come halfway. Just enough to get his hopes up, then Yuri would gun the American down.

Even as Yuri rehearsed his plan in his mind, he saw Ferrell spring from the ground. Then the American did the last thing Yuri expected, he dived headlong at the sleeping Yakov, and Yuri could not fire for fear of hitting Yakov.

Ferrell's shoulder crashed into the sleeping Russian's midsection, bowling the smaller man over. Ferrell ripped the pistol from Yakov's sash and slashed the barrel viciously across the Russian's forehead.

Rolling clear of Yakov, Ferrell pointed the pistol at Yuri and pulled the trigger. Three times he fired, the slugs smashing the giant Russian to the ground.

Fedarov came awake with a start, his hand automatically reaching for his rifle. "Hold it, string bean," Ferrell shouted, swinging the pistol to cover him. "If I were you, I'd leave that rifle be, I'm just itching for a chance to kill you."

Without a word, Fedarov pulled his hand away from

the rifle and climbed to his feet. "Shoot if you wish. You cannot hope to stop the movement. We have made contingency plans."

Catrinia wasn't listening to Fedarov, she was staring at Ferrell. He was marvelous! He'd saved them! Catrinia had been ready to help him, but he'd moved so fast, it was over before she hardly knew it. She wanted to rush to him and throw her arms around him. She didn't, though. Such was not accepted behavior for a lady of her station.

She saw him step back and toe the unconscious body of Yakov. Sure that he was really out cold, Ferrell took a deep breath and smiled at her. Blushing, Catrinia looked down at her hands in her lap.

Just as a warm feeling swept through her body, Catrinia heard a dull thud. Looking up, she saw Ferrell slowly topple facefirst into the ground.

As Ferrell hit the ground, Vladamir stepped into the firelight, holding his rifle, butt forward. "I am sorry to report that in the darkness, I lost the two American brothers," Vladamir said.

A savage smile on his face, Fedarov snatched his rifle off the ground. "A mistake I shall overlook," he said, kicking Yakov. "Wake him," he instructed Vladamir.

As Vladamir struggled to wake Yakov, Fedarov glanced at Yuri and shook his head. "Can no one do anything right?"

The quick reversal of fortune got to Catrinia. The letdown nearly broke her heart and she wanted to cry. Then she remembered the letters to her father. She had to destroy them! Scooping them up, she scrambled for the fire.

Fedarov saw her movements and guessed her intentions. Pivoting, he grabbed her around the waist with one arm and picked her up off the ground, flinging her back. Bending down, he snatched them from her hand. "Thank you, Duchess. You have helped to create a new Russia."

Holding the letters, Fedarov looked to Vladamir and the still groggy Yakov. "We have wasted enough time. Tie them both to that tree," he barked, then began reading.

Catrinia fought them, but Vladamir and Yakov were both powerful men. Aside from bloodying Vladamir's lip, she done them no harm. They forced her against the tree, pulling her arms around behind the tree and tying them tightly.

After she was secured, they dragged the limp body of Ferrell Cauruthers over to the tree beside her and tied him in the same fashion. As he sagged against his bonds, Catrinia could see the blood matted in Ferrell's hair.

"If you believe in God, Czaritsa, I suggest you make peace with him," Fedarov said, without looking up from his reading. "You are going to meet him very soon." Fedarov glanced up at his two men. "Kill them both!"

Yakov and Vladamir took up their rifles and lined up in front of her and Ferrell. As they raised the rifles, Catrinia closed her eyes. When the shots crashed, they were louder than she expected.

Even before the first light of a new day appeared across the land, Bobby Stamper and Louis Claude were up, drinking coffee and munching on hardtack. "I'd like to know what the devil is going on,'' Bobby fumed, as he poured himself another cup. ''Looks like a parade ground out here. I never saw so many tracks in my whole life.''

His face stiff from sleep, Louis yawned and nodded. ''Something is wrong here,'' he agreed, shaking his head to clear the sleep away.

''Them two Russians in town—they're up to something, I can feel it,'' Bobby stated.

Claude shook his head. ''I doubt it. They merely came to see their duchess.''

''Yeah! That's what I mean!'' Bobby shouted, jumping to his feet. ''They traveled all this way and they was talking about what an honor it was to see this princess, but they didn't sound too fired up about the deal. Sounded like they was reading it out of a book.'' Bobby stalked around their camp, drinking his coffee. Suddenly he whirled, stabbing a finger at the Frenchman. ''And when you told them that their princess had been snatched, they never even batted an eye. They acted like they already knew.''

Louis Claude smiled and shook his head. ''You are seeing devils where there are none, my friend. Russians are like that. They are a passionless people. They do not know how to celebrate life or grieve a loss as we French do.''

''I still say they're up to something. I'd bet my bottom dollar on it,'' Bobby maintained. He threw the rest of his coffee on the fire. ''Let's get going. I want to find them kids and get back to town.''

Louis would have liked another cup of coffee, but he knew how impatient Bobby could be. When he was young, Claude had been the same way, but as he grew older, Louis found he liked to linger a bit. Still, Bobby was right—they had to find Stevie and Jenny.

As the sun came up, they found something. It wasn't the kids, it was Lester and Elmo's camp. Bobby jumped off his horse, prowling the camp. "This is weird," he muttered as he studied the tracks. "They came in after the dew set in last night and left before dawn. They built a fire, but didn't do no cooking. They couldn't have been here more than a couple of hours. Maybe less."

"That don't hardly make sense," Claude protested. "Why would anyone build a fire and set up camp for just a couple of hours?"

"That ain't all," Bobby replied. "I'd swear this was Lester and Elmo's camp. I'd recognize them crooked, run-down, homemade boot tracks anywhere."

"Any sign of the kids?" Claude asked.

Scowling at the tracks like he thought they should tell him more, Bobby shook his head. "I'd like to know what the devil is going on. They went back the same way they came. That don't make no sense."

Claude chuckled dryly. "We're talking about Elmo and Lester here. When did them two ever do anything that made sense? Let's just catch them and find out what they did with Stevie and Jenny."

They set out again, stopping just a minute to scratch their heads at Vladamir's tiny camp. They were just leaving, when a ragged volley of shots rang out.

Chapter Twenty

Me and Rostov were still hot on the trail when the sun came up. It hadn't been easy, tracking in the dark, but we'd stuck with it. Had we been looking up instead of down, we might have noticed all the dust clouds riding across the serene sky.

As the light came, I blew out the lamp and started to sit it beside the trail. It didn't seem right to leave a perfectly good lamp behind, so, being careful not to spill the kerosene, I packed the thing in my saddlebag.

Now that we had some light to track by, we covered some ground. This morning, Rostov wasn't saying much; I reckon his shoulder was bothering him. The silence was getting on my nerves. I was hunting my brain for something to say, when all of a sudden, three shots sounded in one rolling boom.

"Those came from close by!" I shouted, slapping the spurs to my horse. I took off like a shot, but Rostov was already ahead of me as we pounded in the direction of them shots. We ran our horses hard, until I figured we were getting close. "We best stop," I hissed up at Rostov.

For once that hardheaded Russian listened to good sense. We dropped off our horses, spreading out as we moved in silently on foot. We could see a small stand of trees ahead, and that's where we were heading. As we neared the tiny grove, I saw a man and woman tied to a pair of trees. Like a firing squad, two men with rifles stood in front of them. Behind them, standing straight and tall, was a fancy-looking jasper.

Now, I figured this was a time to take stock, but not so with Rostov. Hollering something in Russian, he stepped out in the open. Slapping the rifle to his shoulder, he jerked the trigger. Well, sir, that rifle was plumb dry and just went click.

For a second, Rostov just stood there, a stunned expression on his face. Then, of all things, he turned to glare accusingly at me. Those two men with the rifles whirled as one, firing at him. Even from where I was at, I could hear the bullets smash into him and saw him topple to the ground.

The whole thing kinda caught me off guard, and it took me a second to get going. When I did, I centered my rifle on a solid-looking feller. I squeezed the trigger and through my sights saw him flop to the ground.

I swung my rifle to nail another one of them jaspers, but like groundhogs they hit the dirt. Figuring to worry them a mite, I sent a few shots screaming into the dirt around them.

I was plugging some fresh shells in my gun, when I heard a mess of yelling and screaming. "What the devil?" I muttered as I looked back over my shoulder.

After I looked, I wished I hadn't. I saw one of the scariest sights I ever hope to see; Lester and Elmo charging headlong into the fracas. They were waving their pistols and screaming like a couple of drunk banshees. I didn't know what they were doing here, or whose side they were on, I just hoped it wasn't our side.

As they started to run past the prone Rostov, he jumped to his feet. Sticking out a huge arm, he collared Lester around the neck. Poor Lester's feet shot out from underneath him, and he hit the dirt like a sack of oatmeal.

Elmo tried to veer past Rostov, but the big Russian's arms were too long. He bulldogged Elmo, pummeling the smaller man as he rode him to the ground.

Now, all of that was mighty entertaining, and I reckon I got caught up watching it. Well, when that bullet smacked the tree right in front of my face, that jerked me up short. Turning my attention back to the matter at hand, I tried to figure out what to do now. I'd just decided that it was about a standoff, when that fancy jasper called out.

"Rostov, you and your friend throw down your weapons, or we shall kill the duchess."

So that was the duchess. Despite the situation, I was curious and glanced over for a look at the ol' gal. And you know what? She was gone! So was that feller tied with her.

Her and that feller that had been tied to the tree were gone. I guess that fancy feller noticed the same thing, 'cause he half raised up, staring at the empty trees.

Well, when he raised up, I snapped off my shot. I did it without thinking. I nailed him, but not good and solid. My shot spun him around, and as I worked the lever on my rifle, somebody opened up from the other side of the camp.

I didn't have the first idea who was helping us, I was just glad they were. They drilled that fancy jasper and he nosed into the dirt heavily.

Yakov had been hugging the dirt when he saw Fedarov go down. All of a sudden, Yakov realized, he didn't want to be here. Both Fedarov and Vladamir were dead, and Yakov was alone. Jumping to his feet, he took off running.

He heard the shots seeking him, and fear lent speed to his feet. Dodging through the trees, he felt a surge of hope. He was going to make it! He was going to get away!

The feeling of elation sweeping through him was crushed when Ferrell Cauruthers stepped out in front of him. Ferrell was limping, and dried blood covered his neck, but there was nothing wrong with the pistol in his hand.

Yakov tried to stop and bring his rifle to bear, but Ferrell was already firing. "You killed my partner!" Ferrell said as he fired. Ferrell fired until the pistol ran dry. No emotion showed on his face as he watched Yakov crumple to the ground. Looking tired, he dropped the pistol.

I saw that dark feller break and run, and I took off after him. As I ran, I saw two men on horseback break from cover and take up the pursuit. In a glance, I recognized them—Bobby and Mr. Claude.

I glanced at the two bodies as I rushed past them, just to make sure they were dead. When we reached Yakov, he was dead as well; a long lanky man was standing over him.

Right about then, everybody went to talking at once. For a minute, it turned into a regular shouting match, but being a big man, I had the wind power to drown them out. "Who are you?" I asked the lanky man.

"Ferrell Cauruthers," he answered.

"How'd you manage to get untied?"

"I cut them loose."

I glanced over and saw Stevie and Jenny weaving through the trees, a woman with them. When I saw Stevie, my blood went to boiling like a pressure cooker. I tell you, I was mad enough to bite the head off a snapping turtle. I wanted to cut loose on the boy with both barrels, but Bobby beat me to it.

"Stevie!" he exclaimed. "We been looking all over the country for you."

Now, I reckon Stevie had been in trouble enough to know how to act. He hung his head. "Sorry," he mumbled.

"So that's why you happened along!" I said, looking at Bobby and Louis. "What did he do this time?"

"It's a long story," Bobby replied, then pointed a finger at Stevie. "When we get back to town, you're in big trouble," he told the youngster.

"You got that right," I seconded. "I told you to stay put. You coulda got yourself killed."

"They was all watching you," Stevie declared. "No one even looked my way while I was cutting them loose."

Now, how do you argue with that?

Well, I was gonna give it a try. I was just figuring out what to say, when a sweet voice interrupted my thoughts. "Don't be too hard on them. They may have saved our lives," that duchess said.

For this woman, I would've painted every board in Whiskey City and fixed up the place till I was blue in the face. I would've ridden halfway across Wyoming and walked the other half. I would've been shot at and I would've killed for her. I figured it was high time I took a gander at the old gal.

When I finally squared off and looked at her, my mouth like to come off its hinges. She weren't the dried-up, sour old hag I'd been half expecting. No, sir, she was a pretty young lady.

"I am Catrinia Romanov, and I am forever in your debt," she said, offering a dainty little hand. "All of you," she added.

I was shaking her hand when, out of the corner of my eye, I saw Ferrell Cauruthers pick up a pistol from the ground and hand it to Stevie. "Thanks for the loan," he said to the youngster.

We were still pumping hands all around, when we heard a hoarse cry. "Rostov!" I exclaimed.

We took off at a high gallop, and I noticed that princess held back, lending a hand to that Ferrell gent, who had a gimp leg. When we reached Rostov, the big Russian wasn't moving. Trapped underneath him and screaming to high heaven was Elmo.

As we gently rolled Arkady over, Elmo jumped to his feet. "Dang big galoot liked to smoothercated me," Elmo screeched, dabbing at the blood dripping from his nose.

"Shut up," Bobby snapped, drawing his weapon. He herded Elmo over to Lester, who had sat up and was twisting his head from side to side.

"Is Arkady going to be all right?" Catrinia asked as Louis and I went to work on him.

"Yeah, I reckon he'll be fine," I replied and Louis nodded. Rostov had been shot in the thigh and once through the arm. He'd bleed like a geyser, but I figured he'd pull through. As we patched him up, his eyes fluttered open.

"Catrinia? She is safe?" he whispered.

"I'm right here," she said, bending down and taking his hand.

Rostov looked ready to confab a bit, but I stomped on that notion. "You just lie back and rest. It's a fair piece into Whiskey City and you're gonna need your strength."

You know, for once, that mule-headed Russian listened. A smile on his lips, he leaned back and closed his eyes.

Once we'd done all we could for him, Louis went down to check on the men we'd shot. I turned to Bobby, who was still holding a gun on Lester and Elmo. ''What'd they do this time?'' I asked tiredly.

''Tried to rob the bank,'' Bobby replied. ''They didn't get the safe open, but they busted up some of Andrews's fancy doodads.'' Bobby hesitated. ''They also cold-cocked Iris.''

''That there was an accident!'' Lester howled as I groaned.

''Like shooting me was an accident?'' Ferrell Cauruthers asked quietly.

Lester went to bobbing his head like a woodpecker boring a hole and stabbed a shaky finger at Cauruthers. ''Yeah! Zactly like that!''

''You shot him?'' Bobby asked, shaking his head. ''Boys, you got a lot to answer for.''

''I reckon the only fair thing to do is turn them over to Iris,'' I said, trying to keep a straight face,

Elmo's knees went slack, and I thought he was gonna swoon. ''Mercy, no!'' he begged, swaying on his feet.

''Excuse me, gentlemen,'' Catrinia said, stepping between us. ''What if I were to pay restitution for their actions?''

''You want to pay their freight?'' I asked.

''They helped me,'' she said. ''And I promised them a reward.''

''That's right!'' Lester shouted. ''We're gonna get a reward,'' he added, jumping up and down.

Elmo squared his shoulders and snapped his suspenders. "Was my idea to come back and save her," he allowed, like they'd actually been a help.

"Were not!" Lester screamed and promptly shoved his brother into the dirt.

"Teddy! Come quick!" Louis shouted as I was stepping in to separate them.

Something in Louis's tone made the hair on the back of my neck stand up. "That fancy jasper is gone!" he shouted.

"Fedarov!" Cauruthers exclaimed.

We hustled down there, and found that Louis was right. That Fedarov had disappeared like a ghost, and so had Bobby's horse. I guess, while we was fussing over Rostov, Fedarov got up and snuck away.

Holding onto Cauruthers's arm, Catrinia stared at us. "We have to find him! He plans to assassinate my father!" she wailed. "You have to stop him!"

Tears in her eyes, she looked at us all. "Will you help me?"

I reckon that had we any idea what we were letting ourselves in for, we woulda backed away. But we didn't. As one, we stepped up and gave our word to stop this Fedarov.

But that is a tale for another day.